THE FREEDOM FINDERS

Touch
the S

EMILY CONOLAN

D0557209

To Hani, and all the poets who have crossed the seas

Supported by

Tasmanian
Government

First published by Allen & Unwin in 2018

Allen & Unwin
83 Alexander Street Crows Nest NSW 2065 Australia
Phone: (61 2) 8425 0100 Email: info@allenandunwin.com Web: www.allenandunwin.com

 A catalogue record for this
book is available from the
National Library of Australia

ISBN 978 1 76029 492 2

For teaching resources, explore www.allenandunwin.com/resources/for-teachers

Cover design by Karen Scott and Sandra Nobes
Text design by Sandra Nobes and Karen Scott
Set in 11.5 pt Sabon by Sandra Nobes
Photo of Hani Abdile on page 324 © Dominic Lorrimer
Vintage map on pages 330–331 © Lukasz Szwaj / Shutterstock
Photo of author on page 334 © Nick Tompson

This book was printed in Australia in January 2018 by McPherson's Printing Group

10 9 8 7 6 5 4 3 2 1

www.emilyconolan.com.au

AUTHOR'S NOTE

DEAR READER,

I grew up reading 'Choose Your Own Adventure' books by Edward Packard, RA Montgomery and others. I loved making the choices as I read the story, and backtracking through the maze of plots until I found the most satisfying ending. Sometimes I'd end up being eaten by a giant squid; other times, I'd get to save the universe from aliens.

Those books were pure fantasy. The Freedom Finders books are different, because the choices here are based on real events. Although this story is made up, it contains some scenes of violence and difficult choices that shouldn't – but unfortunately do – sometimes happen to real kids like you. If you find anything in this book upsetting to read, make sure you find a trusted adult to talk to about it.

I work as a teacher and refugee advocate. Through this work, I've made many friends who have lived through a refugee's journey: taking enormous risks to escape danger, and eventually making it to safety in Australia. During these journeys, sometimes there was no choice about what would happen next. At other times, these friends faced life-and-death decisions.

Each Freedom Finders book tells the story of a different child from a different generation and place coming to Australia as a migrant or refugee. In my eyes, people who undertake this journey are heroes, and are just as deserving of being the star of a book as any alien-busting dude with superpowers. As you read the series, I hope you will see that the journeys in each book have similar themes running through them: courage, sacrifice and love.

I have never experienced danger like this. My life in Australia has been privileged and comfortable, and I'm thankful for that. I am not a refugee, a Somali person, a Muslim, or a young boy – and you, reader, might not be either – but the character you will become while you read this book is.

So, how did I write this story, when it is not my story? Well, in part I combined the experiences of lots of real people, my imagination, and some memories of grief, triumph and terror from my own life…but it wasn't that simple.

I also worked really closely with my Somali friend Hani Abdile, who came to Australia by boat. Although it's not a retelling of her life story, Hani's journey and her choices had a huge influence on this book, and I worked hard to try to understand them.

That's why I've included an interview with Hani in the back (see pages 324–327), plus Hani's poems on pages 122–123, 265–266, 285–286, 292–293 and 302. Hani is an amazing writer, and I'm certain she has much success ahead of her. Hani, thank you from the bottom of my heart.

I also needed to check I'd got the details in the story right, and that I hadn't accidentally included any culturally sensitive or offensive information, including religious details.

My sincere thanks go, again, to Hani, as well as to another excellent Somali friend, Abdi Aden, and to Nadia Niaz, for checking the story for accuracy before it went to print.

There may still be some places where I got things wrong. In these instances, I can only ask for forgiveness, take criticism on board, and hope that the book still has a positive impact overall.

For details of Hani and Abdi's own books, and ways you can get involved, see page 329.

After reading this book, I hope you will take a look around your own community and notice that there are Freedom Finders everywhere: all sorts of people who push beyond limiting expectations, and create something better. Get curious about the ways people around you seek freedom. Get energised about doing what you can to make sure freedom is extended to all. It's the only way to save the planet from annihilation and be a genuine superhero.

EMILY CONOLAN, 2018

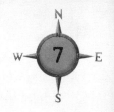

You're about to kick the winning goal for Somalia in the World Cup. Your foot is poised above the ball. The crowds in the stands are roaring your name. The only problem is that the guys you are up against are a team of man-sized scorpions carrying AK-47s, and you're worried that if they lose, they might eat you for revenge.

One voice seems to be shouting your name more loudly than all the others. 'Wake up!' it calls. Aunty Rahama shakes your shoulder. The crowds and the scorpions fade away. You sit up groggily.

The three of you – Aunty Rahama, you and your little sister, Jamilah – share a narrow bed in the back room of a grocery shop. Light filters in from the gaps around the edges of the tin roof, and the orange cloth curtain shifts in the breeze. You can hear the shopkeeper preparing for business out the front. Rahama fetches clothes from the cardboard box under the bed, and goes out the back into the alleyway to splash herself under the cold tap.

'Up you get,' she calls, businesslike as ever. 'You too, Jamilah.'

Jamilah's curly black hair is the only part of her poking out from under the sheet. She groans and rolls like a baby warthog in the dust. Aunty Rahama hauls you both out of bed. You wash, then each kneel on your prayer mat to perform morning prayers. Then Rahama wraps her red hijab over her hair, opens up her backpack from work and, with careful pride, clips a small black microphone to the red fabric near her chin.

'Whassat?' asks Jamilah, rubbing her eyes.

'My new microphone. It's so much smaller. It records everything on here.' Rahama lifts up her top a little and points to a black box she has clipped to the waistband of her cotton trousers.

'I want to come with you two today,' says Jamilah.

'Not yet, chickpea. It's too risky. When you're bigger.'

Soon you and Rahama step outside into the blazing morning light. Overhead, seagulls from Lido Beach wheel through the blue sky. Cars honk, bicycles weave, and an old man herds goats down the street to market.

A couple of doors down from your place, a young man sits in the doorway with a guitar, strumming some chords and humming. The simple melody gives you goosebumps all over.

A month ago, when the terrorist group al-Shabaab was everywhere in the city, the man could have been killed for daring to do this. Music, dancing and sport were all forbidden. Even now, with al-Shabaab still in control in some northern outskirts of the city, it's still a brave, defiant thing to do.

You look closely. The man's face looks ordinary, but now you know he's a secret hero and that his guitar is his weapon.

Rahama turns back to Mr Jabril, the shopkeeper, who's standing in the doorway with Jamilah. 'Thank you for having her,' she says, and then sternly to Jamilah: 'Remember to help Mr Jabril all you can.'

Jamilah sticks out her bottom lip and looks mutinous, but to no avail, because today you and Aunty Rahama have a job to do. You're going out to do your favourite thing: story-hunting.

Aunty Rahama has fought with every bit of courage she has to raise you and Jamilah alone since your hooyo and aabe were killed – and to get her job at the radio station as a journalist.

When you were younger, you hated how she left you to watch Jamilah while she ran off at crazy hours, to follow the sound of shooting, or go to the airport to interview someone important getting off a plane. But now that you're thirteen and Jamilah is eight, Rahama has started to teach you how she does her job, bringing you along on some of the safer stories to hold her equipment – and you're hooked.

'What's the story today?' you ask her as you walk down the road together. It's a busy Saturday morning. The air smells like onion curry from the street vendor on the corner. After you've walked a few more blocks, you reach the intersection where a mortar bomb went off two months ago. The main target is still a blackened hole, but some of the nearby shops that were damaged look like they're about to reopen for business already. The owner of the hot bread shop is giving his freshly laid bricks a bright coat of pink paint.

'How do you know whether Mogadishu is a safe place to live again?' asks Rahama. She likes to tease out a story by challenging your thoughts. You look up and down the bustling street. You think of the man playing his guitar.

'I don't know,' you reply, 'because it's never been really safe – not since before the civil war started, when Hooyo and Aabe were teenagers and you were just a toddler. Even you don't remember that.'

'It seems pretty good now, though, right?' She nods to an AMISOM peacekeeping soldier in a dappled green-and-brown uniform standing on a corner. His hand rests on a long, black gun. 'Now that Barcelona is here to protect us.'

You smile. This codename system's used everywhere in Somalia: people refer to al-Shabaab as the football team 'Arsenal', and now AMISOM has been dubbed the rival team 'Barcelona'. It's safer to be overheard talking about football than terrorism.

'It does seem good now,' you agree, 'but there have been short times of peace in the past, and then the war has started again. How do we know this isn't one of those times? Arsenal might have been kicked out of almost all of Mogadishu for now, but they still control the countryside.'

'And they're still hidden here in the rest of the city, too,' agrees Rahama. 'Just biding their time, like a snake waiting for a rat to cross its path. But where are they hiding...and when will they strike? That's what we don't know. That's why we're still not safe. That's the story.'

You know this street – your whole neighbour-hood – so well that you think you could walk it blindfolded and not step into any of the holes in the broken pavement. But today, something is missing.

'Hang on,' you say to Rahama. You stop in your tracks. 'The lime-seller's not there.'

Close to the end of the street, a little old lady

always sells limes spread out on flattened cardboard boxes. She is blind in one eye and wrinkled like a walnut. She sells the limes there because it's not far from where the fishers bring their boats in, and everyone knows limes go well with fish. She's so old that if you stopped to talk to her she could probably tell you the history of the whole of Somalia, since the British and Italians were here. But today, she's gone. Why?

'Does it matter that the lime lady's not here?' Rahama shrugs.

'I think it does,' you say. 'It feels weird. She was even selling limes the morning after that mortar strike blew apart half the road, remember? So why isn't she here today?'

'Is this a hunch?' Rahama teases you. 'Are you such a professional journalist that you get *hunches* now?'

You ignore her teasing. 'I think we should try to find her,' you say. 'If we're supposed to be doing a story on how Mogadishu is changing and whether it's safe, she'd be the perfect person to ask – she's seen everything on these streets.'

Rahama agrees to your plan. You ask some of the other street vendors where the lime lady has gone, but they seem reluctant to say anything.

'Don't go looking for trouble,' warns a woman selling matches and soap from a cardboard box strung around her neck. 'Allah knows, that poor old woman has enough to deal with.'

The baby tied to the woman's back starts to cry, and the woman looks nervously up and down the street before hurrying away.

You offer a little boy a biscuit if he'll show you the way to the lime-seller's house, and he eagerly leads you and Rahama down streets, through dirt paths lined with weeds, and into the bombed-out ruin of what used to be a theatre overlooking the sea.

The building looks like a long-ago giant bit the top off it, crunched it up, then spat it back out. The walls are grey and crumbling concrete, laced with bullet marks. Weeds and twisted metal guard the entranceway, but you can see a little foot track leading inside, and someone has dragged a large sheet of corrugated metal over the top of one section of the ruin for a roof.

Your little guide points inside the ruin. You hand him his biscuit and he scampers away, crumbs around his mouth.

'Hello?' you call tentatively. 'Anyone there?'

Behind you, you hear a slight *click* as Rahama switches on her microphone.

Suddenly, a thin, weathered hand shoots out from the shadows, and pulls you and Rahama through the entranceway and into the ruin.

'I know you!' hisses a voice. Your eyes take a moment to adjust to the dim light. It's the lime lady, her one blind eye wandering and milky, her good eye beadily sizing you up. 'You're the boy who lives out the back of the grocery shop, and his journalist aunty. I'm not selling limes today. Get lost.'

You hear a groan behind her and squint into the gloom. In the corner of the ruin, lying on a bed made of the same cardboard boxes the lady uses to sell her fruit on, is a man – and the sight of him makes you want to scream and run.

Rahama gasps – she's seen him too. The man's eyes are puffed and purple as plums, and half his mouth is a bloody mess, with teeth cracked like splintered wood. He's been really badly beaten up.

He tries to sit up, and his body shakes with the effort. You see that one of his legs has been bandaged with scraps of cloth and newspaper. The lime lady moves to stand protectively in front of him.

'Who are you?' Rahama asks the man. 'Who did this to you?'

'Get lost,' repeats the lime lady. 'Forget you ever saw us.'

'Please,' insists Rahama, 'he needs proper medical help!' She fishes a crumpled note from her pocket and gives it to you. 'Run to the market,' she commands, 'and get bandages, antiseptic and painkillers. Quick.'

You sprint through the streets and buy the items. By the time you return, your calf muscles are burning. You duck under the tin roof, and the lime lady rises from her small cooking fire in the corner. Rahama is leaning towards the beaten-up man, her face gripped with concentration as he begins his story.

You hand the medical supplies to the lime lady, surprised to see tears of gratitude in her eyes. 'Zayd is my only son,' she whispers. 'But he's in grave danger.'

You can see that it hurts Zayd to talk – his voice hisses around his broken teeth – but he struggles on.

'I was a unit commander with al-Shabaab,' he is saying. 'I was very high up in the ranks. I thought they could bring law and order to Somalia. I believed that what they did was justified. But then...' He heaves a rattling breath and puts a hand to his broken ribs. 'Then they brought me a new group of trainees, about six weeks ago. They were so young. How old are you, boy?' he asks, turning to you for the first time.

'I'm thirteen.'

'They looked much the same age as you. Scared, skinny. Some of them were trying to pretend they knew what was going on, but…they had no idea. My orders were to give them basic training in how to shoot a gun, then send them to the frontlines of the fighting in Mogadishu. Those boys were just bait: to be thrown out for AMISOM to shoot at, while more of our troops moved in behind.'

The lime lady takes the bloody wrapping from her son's leg. You have to look away as the bandages come off the maroon wound.

'Do you know where the boys came from?' asks Rahama.

'They were orphans, all of them. They came from the same place: Bright Dream Orphanage. A false name for a terrible place. The things I could tell you about Bright Dream … but I'll get to that.' He sighs.

The lime lady wraps her son's leg in a clean bandage. She begins to pace around the front of their home, wringing her bony hands. There is a rustle from something in the corner – probably a rat – and she jumps.

If it's true that her son has run away from his job with al-Shabaab, you know she won't be able to keep him hidden for long before al-Shabaab return and exact their revenge. You start to feel very nervous, and the dim, stuffy room in the ruin begins to feel airless as Zayd continues with his story.

'I didn't want to, but I followed orders and sent the boys into battle,' he says.

His voice has become slower, and every word seems to cause him pain.

'I stood by and watched them go off to fight, day after day. At night, they barely slept – just sat there with a horrible, faraway look in their eyes, or sometimes woke screaming from a nightmare. By the end of the second week of fighting, nearly all of them had been killed. But some were wounded: superficial bullet wounds, a broken arm, things that would heal. I asked permission for them to rest and to be treated. These boys had been so brave. But instead, they told me to…to…'

'What did they tell you to do?' asks Rahama.

'They told me to kill all the injured ones,' stutters the man. He holds his head in his hands. 'Can you imagine? They said, *We don't have the time and money to treat rats. Stop being their nurse and just shoot them. They're worthless.*'

You feel a cold shudder run through you. These were boys your own age – orphans like you, but without an Aunty Rahama to keep them safe.

'I said, *You can't ask me to shoot my own troops.*

I thought you followed Allah's law, but this is an abomination. You can't kill these boys like animals.'

Zayd sighs again, and his mother stops pacing a moment to rest her hand on his shoulder.

'That was when they started beating me,' he says. 'They left me for dead.'

You hear a crunch of footsteps coming through the rubble and weeds outside. Everyone in the room stiffens.

'Zayd!' shouts a voice. 'Zayd Tarabi, come and face us!'

You look at Aunty Rahama, stricken. You will both be killed along with Zayd if al-Shabaab finds you here.

'Quick!' snaps the lime lady. 'Into the hole!' With the strength of a fit young person, the tiny, wizened lady drags a piece of concrete to one side to reveal a hidey-hole in the floor. 'Get in!'

You, Rahama and Zayd squirm down into the hole. The lime lady shoves the concrete back over the gap, raining pebbles and dust down onto you. You are compressed into a black stew of elbows and breathing and uncomfortable wriggles.

The lime lady bravely stays above ground. 'I'm his mother,' you hear her cry, as heavy boot-steps enter the room. 'He isn't here. Go away!'

'Then whose are these bloody rags on the floor?' snarls a voice. 'Bandages for your injured son who isn't home, perhaps?'

You curse silently. Nobody hid the evidence of Zayd, and now it's right under their noses.

'I have to tell you about Bright Dream,' Zayd whispers, 'before I die.'

You can tell from his voice that he is struggling to breathe from the pain of climbing into the hole with his broken bones and the crush of your bodies next to him.

'Bright Dream's not an orphanage,' he goes on, so softly you can barely make out the words. 'It's the key to al-Shabaab's downfall. You have to tell the world what they're doing there—'

A scream from the lime lady cuts Zayd short. 'Let go of me!' she cries. 'I tell you, he's not here!'

Zayd's body is tense and bristling like a cornered dog. You know he won't be able to hide in this hole and listen to his mother being hurt. How could he?

'I have to stop them,' Zayd mutters. 'I have to try. Remember: investigate Bright Dream.'

He pushes the concrete above your heads to one side. The room immediately falls silent. You and Rahama are still out of sight as Zayd clambers up through the small gap he's made.

'You have me,' he gasps, his voice tight with the pain of moving. 'Now put her down.'

The lime lady lets out a sob. You're trying not to choke from all the dust in the hole. You can see Rahama's wide eyes shining in the dim light slanting down through the gap. She places a hand on your wrist: *Stay here. Hide.*

A powerful, wild heat pumps through your limbs.

Should you stay hidden in the hole, and let the men from al-Shabaab take Zayd? They will almost certainly kill him. But at least you and Rahama will survive, and go on to investigate his story.

Or should you make a surprise attack: leap from the hole and try to rescue Zayd? It sounds like there are at least two men in the room above. They will certainly have guns, and you don't have a weapon. But you have the element of surprise. Could it possibly work?

✦ If you jump out of the hole and try to rescue Zayd, turn to page 21.

✦ If you stay hidden, turn to page 26.

✦ To read a fact file on Somalia, turn to page 304, then return to this page to make your choice.

You scramble upwards, out of the hole. Rahama's hand snatches at your ankle and you hear her hiss, '*No!*' but you kick her away and leap from hiding.

Two men whirl to face you: one of them is holding Zayd by the throat, and the other one immediately drops Zayd's mother and reaches for his weapon.

You run at the man reaching for his gun, and throw your full body weight into his chest. He stumbles, and out of the corner of your eye, you see the lime lady reach down to her little cooking fire and grab a hot pot of tea. She smashes it into the man's head, and he screams as scalding tea runs down his face. You try to snatch at his gun, and the two of you tussle for control of the weapon.

Rahama has now also climbed from the hole. She picks up a chunk of broken concrete and charges at the man holding Zayd. She is aiming to smash the block of concrete against his head, but he throws out one arm and shoves her sideways into the wall.

The man you are wrestling with gets his finger to the trigger and fires indiscriminately. Chunks of concrete burst open at your feet, and the sound deafens you.

With ringing and dim shouting in your ears, you see Rahama holding her leg and trying not to cry. Blood is rising between her fingers and beginning to soak her clothes. Zayd manages to get free of his captor, but, unsteady on his broken leg, a single punch to the jaw unbalances him and he slams into the ground at your feet.

The lime lady, defiant to the last, is calling the men every horrible name she can think of. 'You dogs! You savage, ignorant, flea-bitten dogs of hell! You child-murderers! You poisonous snakes!'

One of the men uses the butt of his rifle to knock her out, and she crumples to the floor.

The men grab you and Zayd by the throats and begin to drag you from the room. You kick and fight the man who has hold of you, but he is so much bigger – you may as well try to punch a boulder.

Zayd is gasping: 'Leave the boy! He's done nothing wrong! It's me you came for. Just leave him be!'

Rahama is pleading too: 'Stop! Put him down! Take me instead!'

The men don't reply, and when Rahama staggers after them, they push her to the ground.

The men bind and gag you and Zayd and toss you both into the back of their van, like goats to be slaughtered. You bump away from the ruin, past Lido Beach and through Mogadishu.

An hour later, you are rattling through the desert, your limbs crying out to be loosed from the ropes.

Where are they taking us? you wonder. *Why haven't they killed us yet?*

You wonder if you are being taken away for training, to end up on the frontlines of an unwinnable battle, like the boys from Bright Dream Orphanage did before you. Then suddenly – *wham!*

The car hits a pothole and veers off the road. The world flips, and ground and sky whirl past the windows. Your body ricochets off the floor, windows, car seats, and the ceiling. Up is down, and down is up. Smashed glass and rocks fly through the air; your body is being thumped from every direction.

With a final *crunch* and a hiss, the car comes to a standstill. You are buried underneath the body of one of the al-Shabaab men. His blood is trickling down onto you. The other man, the driver, is slumped over the steering wheel, not moving.

As you struggle to get free, you see Zayd sit up. Still gagged, he manages to free himself from the ropes that bind him. He climbs out of a jagged hole in the van's smashed window and begins to stumble away from the wreckage.

'Zayd!' you try to shout. 'Zayd, I'm alive! Help me!' You are still gagged, but you make enough of a noise that he turns and notices you.

He starts to hobble back towards the vehicle to save you. He stretches out a hand. Just at that moment, you hear a *boom* as the petrol tank ignites. A ball of flame throws Zayd backwards.

You struggle against the heavy man on top of you, but the flames and the smoke are too much, and you collapse.

You feel as though your soul is rising out of your body so that you can look down on the bonfire wreckage where your body lies burning. Zayd staggers away from the scene. You saved his life, but his chances of survival as a man with broken bones in the middle of the desert are slim.

Your soul seems to rise even higher, and you can see the city of Mogadishu. You can even see the ruined theatre by the sea, where two women sit crying. Your Aunty Rahama has revived the lime lady; next she will struggle home despite the bullet wound in her leg, determined to find out what happened to you and to investigate the mystery of Bright Dream Orphanage.

You float away from the earth, the coastline of Somalia now coming into view, like a silver thread on the edge of a ragged skirt. You can still see the orange spot where the car burns in the desert. It's just a pinprick of brilliant light.

Then you are gone.

THE END

✳ To return to your last choice and try again, go to page 20.

No, you reason. *Even with the element of surprise, an attack could never work.*

You've lived in a war zone your whole life – you've seen gunfights and dead bodies – and it's made you very realistic about the chances of a thirteen-year-old boy against two fully grown, armed men. Besides which, Aunty Rahama is gripping your wrist so tightly your fingers are starting to tingle. There's nothing to do but sit in the hole and wince.

There are doughy thuds and scraping sounds from above, and the lime lady's quiet sobs, as Zayd is thrown to the ground, tied up and dragged away. Then, suddenly, there's a shout – Zayd's voice.

'*Cross the river on the banner of the eagle!*' he yells with all his strength. Then an engine roars into life, and he is gone.

YOU LIE AWAKE that night thinking about those words. What did he mean? Was it a clue? How will you find out what Zayd meant? How must the lime lady feel tonight, all alone in the ruin, without her son?

You and Aunty Rahama didn't tell Jamilah what happened, because you don't want to scare her. But in the darkness, Rahama's hand finds yours, and you know she is lying awake thinking of it all too.

'We promised the lime lady we'd investigate Zayd's story,' you whisper. 'But how can we even hope to make a difference? He's probably already...'

You can't bring yourself to say the word 'dead'.

'Sometimes I wonder if I'm making a difference,' Rahama murmurs. 'On the dark days, I think, *What's the point? I'm risking my life trying to bring justice to a country hell-bent on war and revenge. Will anyone even care?*'

She sighs.

'We've lost so many freedoms in this country. Our family was taken away from us – and our country's riches, and our peaceful society. We were left with so little, but we still have our words. The voices of Somali people have survived colonisation, dictatorships, twenty years of civil war, and a fundamentalist takeover. Whatever other freedoms they may have stolen from us, I will not let them take my voice. Never. The truth can kill Arsenal faster than any bullet.'

'But what do you think *Cross the river on the banner of the eagle* means?' you ask.

'I don't know,' confesses Rahama. 'But you and I are going to find out.'

THAT MONDAY, RAHAMA insists that you and Jamilah go to school. You want to go to work with her and help, but you know that no amount of begging will change her mind.

Your school only reopened a couple of weeks ago, after the most recent fighting died down. You've been working hard to try to catch up on your missed education. At least Aunty Rahama, being well educated, has been able to keep teaching you and Jamilah to read and write in Somali and Arabic anytime the school's closed down. She's also taught you all the English she knows, since so many journalists around the world use it.

After school, you're walking home with Jamilah along a busy street when suddenly Rahama appears from behind a shop and drags you down an alley. She wraps her arms around you and draws you both in close. She's sweaty and breathless.

'Things have changed,' Rahama whispers urgently. 'Arsenal are onto me – they know about my interview with Zayd, and they know that I know about Bright Dream. Don't panic, though,' she whispers to you, as you feel horror rise inside you. 'They don't know *you* were there, my darling. There's no reason for them to come after you. All right?'

You nod mutely, squeezing Jamilah to your side. You feel her shoulders trembling.

'I need you to do something,' Aunty Rahama goes on, looking you square in the eye. 'If I don't come home tonight…'

For just a moment, her face wavers, as though it's about to collapse. Are those tears in her eyes? Then she draws herself up and leans in again. Her voice is choked and fierce with love.

'If I don't come home tonight, your first job is to look after Jamilah. That's more important than anything else. Your second job is to take our story to a safe place.'

She pushes an object into your hands. It is a pen made of solid gold, shining in the sunlight. The writing tip is sharp as a sword, and at the other end a single ruby twinkles like a pomegranate seed.

'What's this?' Jamilah whispers in awe.

Rahama unscrews the pen and shows you a secret memory stick hidden inside.

'Wow!' you gasp.

She quickly screws the pen closed again. 'It's the recording of the interview we did with Zayd. It's the only other copy in existence, besides my file. There's a note under my pillow that will explain everything. But I don't want you to worry, okay? Sometimes you've got to do things that...' She sighs. 'Tough things. But they're for the best. I hope you'll understand why, one day. Just remember, I'll always be with you both. Never lose hope.'

'Rahama, wait!' you cry. She's turned around and is walking away from you, fast.

Jamilah is clinging to you, tearful. 'Where's Aunty Rahama going?' she asks. 'What was she talking about?'

You think fast. Rahama's in danger. You have to follow her – but you can't bring Jamilah.

Your friend Mahadi walks by, and you grab his arm.

'Mahadi! Can you do something for me? I've got to...run an errand for my aunty. Can you take Jamilah home safely?'

Jamilah starts crying loudly. 'No! No!' she shouts.

Mahadi looks worried. 'Is everything okay?'

You don't have time to explain, and you can't risk sharing Rahama's secret with your friend. 'It's fine,' you lie. You turn to Jamilah. Her hijab has slipped back off her hair, so you tug it back up, wipe her tears and squeeze her shoulders. 'I'll come back,' you promise her. 'Just go home with Mahadi and wait. I promise I'll come back.'

As you slip the pen into your pocket and turn to sprint after Rahama, you hope desperately that it's a promise you will be able to keep.

YOU RUN HARDER and longer than you ever have before, following glimpses of Rahama's red hijab as she crosses busy roads, weaves between shops, and hurries down long streets and around corners.

You're just in time to see her red scarf disappear into the broadcasting building where she works. You run up to the door, but it's locked. That's strange. Why would she lock the door behind her?

Just then, a man pushes past you. He has a gaunt face and a beard flecked with grey. He's dressed in black, and he has a backpack slung over one shoulder. He also tries the door.

'It's locked,' you say, wondering who this man

is. Then he turns to face you and you stifle a gasp, because you recognise him: his name is Qasim, and he used to work in the grocery shop you live behind. He wanted to marry Aunty Rahama, but she wasn't interested.

He's changed from a playful young man into some sort of a ghoul – a shadow with bones. His skin is waxy and his eyes look narrow and lifeless. Not a flicker of expression crosses his face as he glances at you.

You duck your head and walk away quickly, hoping he hasn't recognised you. Then you hide behind a parked car and watch.

Qasim stalks once around the building, then stands outside the front, looking up at it. Suddenly, you see what has caught his eye: the back of a red hijab just near one of the first-floor windows.

Qasim moves until he is directly beneath that window. He slips his backpack down and hides it behind a rubbish bin right under Rahama's window. Then he walks away from the building. He looks neither left nor right. He doesn't hurry. He just slips one hand inside his pocket and walks away, like a man who knows exactly what he's doing.

You can only guess that Rahama's about to start broadcasting your interview with Zayd. You can only guess why someone might deliberately leave a backpack by the broadcasting building right before a major story comes out. Both of those guesses lead to a terrible conclusion.

You run to where the backpack is hidden and, with sweating hands, carefully tug the zip open.

What you see makes your stomach flip: three used Coke cans, held together with black electrical tape; some looping yellow and red wires; and a battery and phone, also strapped on with more tape.

It's a homemade bomb. When Qasim calls the number of the phone that's attached to it, he will trigger a massive explosion.

Your blood thumps in your ears. You want to flee, but you force yourself to breathe and look at the bomb. Your friend Mahadi's family has an electronic repairs shop, so you've seen the inside workings of lots of gadgets before.

This bomb is less complicated than your average toaster. You can see the wires going into the power source. If you lift the tape and unhook those wires then there will be no charge, so the phone call won't work – the bomb won't explode. Easy. Except that if you're wrong... you're dead.

You could get away instead and try to warn

Rahama – but would she hear you and get out of the building in time? And what if Qasim is still somewhere nearby, hears your shout, and comes after you?

You have only seconds to decide.

* To try to defuse the bomb, go to page 35.

* To try to raise the alarm from a distance, turn to page 52.

* To read a fact file on journalists at risk, go to page 307, then return to this page to make your choice.

You use your nail to lift a corner of the tape that binds the bomb together. You know you can defuse it. You just hope you can do it fast enough.

Sweat is making your hands slip on the plastic tape, so you wipe them on your shorts. Then you peel back the tape again, trying to move as steadily and quickly as you can, because if Qasim calls the phone before you get those wires off the bomb, both you and Rahama – not to mention everyone else who happens to be nearby – will die.

The tape is tacky, gluey – your fingers are sticking to it. You ball it up to get it out of the way, then give one more little tug and see the wires connecting to the battery. *Yes.*

You are praying under your breath, verses from the Qur'an, to help steady you and guide you as you begin to untwist the wires, when – *slam!*

You are knocked sideways onto the ground, but not by a bomb blast. Qasim has found you. His knees are on your chest. You feel your ribs bending to cracking point under the pressure. Qasim leans over you. The whites of his eyes are yellow.

'I know you,' he says slowly. 'Rahama's nephew. Trying to play the hero, huh?'

He spits in your face. The warm liquid trickles over your cheek and into one ear. You twist your head uselessly.

Qasim lifts a phone out of his pocket. You think that he's going to ring the number of the phone strapped to the bomb, and you pray you got the wires loose enough in time, but instead, he speaks into it.

'I have someone useful here. The target's nephew.'

Allah, save me, you think. You don't want to be *useful* to al-Shabaab. You want to be no one to them.

You struggle under Qasim's knees until two men come and throw you into the back of a white van.

They lean into the van and use black electrical tape to strap your wrists together behind your neck, then your ankles together. Then they loop rope behind you between your wrists and ankles and tighten it, pulling you back like a bow ready to fire.

The van roars off. Every jolt of the road sends shooting pains through your limbs. The plastic floor of the van, now slick with your sweat, knocks against your head as the shadows of buildings flicker past. You think of Jamilah waiting at home for you, and tears start sliding into your ear. You think of Rahama, and your heart pounds even harder with hot, useless panic.

You feel something digging into your thigh through your pocket. It's the golden pen. You'd forgotten you had it. It's the very thing that al-Shabaab is trying to kill Rahama for, and it's in your pocket.

Just then, you hear a *boom*. The van is still close enough that it seems to bounce as the blast wave hits. The air fills with screams, and with the grinding, crunching sound of a building collapsing.

Rahama.

The driver revs the van harder. There is a riot of honking, and panicked faces flash past the windows.

Hate bubbles up in you like vomit. 'You scum!' you scream. 'You bastards! I'll kill you!'

One of your captors turns around, tips down his sunglasses, looks at you and snorts.

The other one, driving the van, chuckles. 'The little cockroach is angry,' he mocks.

'Because we killed his Aunty Cockroach,' teases the man with the sunglasses in a singsong voice.

'I think there's a baby sister cockroach, too...isn't there? The small ones are easy to squash,' muses the driver.

You thrash and fight like a fish on a hook. You scream until your throat feels rough and dry, even though Sunglasses presses a gun to your head and tells you to shut up. You use every swear word you know.

Your limbs are burning, your muscles tearing from straining so hard against the ropes. The anger burning you up is stronger than the sun. You can feel it curling your insides like they're paper on a fire. When the van eventually stops, you are ready to attack the first person who comes near you.

You hope that, if today is your day to die, it will happen quickly.

Instead, when the van door rolls open, a white-bearded man leans over you in gentle concern.

'Oh, dear, look at this poor boy. You've been too rough with him,' he chides as the two kidnappers slope off.

Through the van door, you see that you're in an unfamiliar suburb of Mogadishu, on a quiet, dusty street. The kidnappers disappear inside a white house with its windows boarded over.

White Beard sets a can of lemon soda on the floor of the van, just near your head. You can see the dew beading on the shiny can. In spite of yourself, your mouth waters.

'I do apologise,' White Beard says, and he carefully cuts your ropes. His voice is mellow and sincere. 'I explained that you are not our enemy, but it seems they overdid it. Are you all right?'

He helps you to sit, and raises the soda to your lips. It is sweet, bubbly heaven in your mouth. He uses the sleeve of his white cotton shirt to wipe your brow.

'Please come inside.'

The driver of the van bows to White Beard as he shepherds you inside. Your mind reels.

White Beard seems to be the leader of this terrorist cell, so he must have planned the bomb that killed Aunty Rahama – yet he seems so kind and steady, like the grandpa you never knew. Is he softening you up for torture? Or is this situation somehow not what you think it is?

White Beard shows you into a room. There is a single bare mattress on the floor, a fluorescent light bulb and no windows. The walls are apple-green. One wall has a black-and-gold-framed hanging of Arabic calligraphy. Your Arabic isn't as fluent as your Somali, and the calligraphy is ornate, but you can make it out: 'There is no power and no strength except with Allah.'

'You killed Aunty Rahama,' you croak. You mean

it to sound like an accusation, but it comes out like a bleat, a question.

Power and strength with Allah, you remind yourself. *Toughen up and stay smart!*

But hot tears spring to your eyes as White Beard sits beside you on the mattress and puts his arm around your shoulders.

'Poor boy, I know the grief must be terrible for you at this moment,' he murmurs. 'But in time, we hope that you will come to understand that Allah has a greater purpose for you – that He can give you light and guidance when you follow His path.'

'I know what Allah's path for me is,' you say, strength returning to your voice. 'It's to become a journalist like my aunty, and to—'

You stop short. You almost said *to investigate Bright Dream*, but of course you don't want to give away that you know anything about that.

'To help Somalia be free,' you finish uncertainly.

'You will only know true freedom when you learn to obey Allah's law,' murmurs White Beard.

'What law is that?' you challenge him. 'Because my aunty taught me the Qur'an inside out, and there isn't anything there about killing people just because they're saying something you don't like.'

White Beard ignores your rising temper. 'We

want you to undertake our training and join al-Shabaab,' he says. 'For one so young, you have great courage and intelligence. We believe you have access to sources and information that will be of use to us.'

You feel Rahama's golden pen pressing into your leg. Surely *this* is the information they're looking for. They'd love to know about this copy of Rahama's interview with Zayd, and the information you have about Bright Dream – even though that isn't much yet. And if they think they can talk you into joining them, they will use you as a soldier in their war. You have to get out of here.

You must choose your next words carefully. You have something that you know they want very much. Perhaps you could use the pen as a bargaining chip – tell them you will give it to them if they'll set you free.

Or perhaps you should keep it hidden, pretend to play along with their plans to undertake training, and look for a way to escape later.

<hr />

✦ To offer the pen in exchange for your freedom, go to page 47.
✦ To wait and look for a way to escape, go to page 42.

I can't give up the pen yet, you tell yourself. *I'm sure I can find another way to escape.*

You turn to White Beard and say, 'All right. If you think it's Allah's will, then I'll stay. I hope I can be useful to you, sir.'

You even make a little bow, hoping you aren't overdoing it, but White Beard seems pleased.

'Good,' he says. 'Very good. I'll get the men to bring you some dinner.'

He rises and leaves the room. You hear a *click* as he locks the door behind him.

Hours later, your two kidnappers bring you a plate of goat stew and rice.

'Can I use the bathroom, please?' you ask.

You're hoping to get out of your room, see more of the house and look for a way to escape. Perhaps you'll even be able to break out of the bathroom. But instead, they bring you a bucket.

'Use that,' the driver says and throws it at you. The door locks again.

You think while you eat the spicy, meaty stew. What can you use to help you? You have a plate, but no cutlery – you're eating with your fingers, like usual. You have a bucket, a mattress, the picture on the wall and, of course, your secret pen.

You have an idea! You use the sharp nib of the pen to stab a little crack into the bottom of the bucket. Then you gobble the rest of your meal and wee into the bucket. As you'd hoped, it starts leaking. Then, for good and stinky measure, you stick your fingers down your throat and vomit into the bucket too. It's a shame to chuck up that goat stew, but you want to make a really awful mess.

You shout at the top of your voice: 'Help! The bucket's leaking!' Just before one of your captors comes to the door, you think to grab a handful of vomit and smear it over your chest. Then as the door opens, you cry out, 'Oh, my stomach! It must have been that stew!'

Standing in the doorway, Sunglasses looks horror-struck. 'Disgusting!' he shouts. The room has a thick, rancid smell to it now, and he gags a little.

You push the bucket towards him and cry, 'Please, take it to the toilet!'

He pushes it back at you angrily and shouts, 'I'm not touching that! Take it to the toilet yourself – and wash yourself while you're in there!'

The bathroom is tacked onto the side of the house,

and luckily it has no ceiling at all – it's a pit in the ground enclosed by concrete walls. You splash a little water onto your face and vomit-covered shirt. You'd better be quick, before they come and check on you.

By standing on the upside-down bucket, you're tall enough to hook your fingers over the top of the wall and scrabble up. You sit astride the wall and scan the area. There's a stray dog lurking below, but no other signs of life. How will you keep that dog distracted? You can't have it barking and alerting everyone.

You scramble back down into the bathroom, lift up the overturned bucket, and grab a handful of your vomit from the ground beneath it, feeling nauseous. This is so disgusting that it just might work.

Using only one hand, you scramble back up the wall; then you toss the sloppy handful of vomit down to the ground. The dog runs over and starts gobbling it up as if it's the yummiest thing it's seen all week. Regurgitated goat. You shudder and wipe your hand on your shorts, and then you leap.

Your feet pound the ground. You wait for the shouts of your captors, but all you can hear are cats fighting, the muffled cry of a cranky baby inside a nearby house, and your own urgent, rhythmic breaths. You run as hard as you can, picking directions at random, just trying to put distance between you and the al-Shabaab house.

Unwanted images flash through your mind. The bomb inside the backpack. Qasim's face as he spat on you. The red hijab at the window.

You begin to stumble. Running so fast right after you've vomited is making you feel wobbly. You slow to a jog, keeping to the shadows, looking for a landmark you recognise. It is a moonlit night. The buildings tower over you like craggy cliffs. Every building is riddled with bullet holes, which tonight look like black shadowy pits on the buildings' ghostly faces.

I'll be leaving you soon, Mogadishu, you think. You don't know how, but you'll have to take Jamilah and go somewhere else – somewhere you can't be found. *You're broken and dangerous*, you think, *but I'll still miss you.*

This city is the only home you've ever known. You'll miss the colourful displays of fruit in the grocery shop at the front of your house; the orange curtains and the rumble of the ocean. You'll miss the minarets of the beautiful mosques, which poke the skyline, and the singsong call to prayer that rings from them five times a day.

You wish that you'd seen Mogadishu in its glory

days, long before the civil war began, when it was one of the most profitable and cosmopolitan trading ports in the world.

People flocked here to buy and sell cloth, spices, paper from Egypt and gold from Sudan, says Rahama's voice, the echo of a memory. *Sailing ships plied the harbour, and every night was filled with feasting and music.*

You stop. You can hear your breath heaving in and out, but there is a second rhythm behind it – the crashing breath of the ocean. Waves!

You follow the sound, and there, silhouetted against the silver sea, is the ruined theatre. You know where you are! With a new burst of energy, you sprint the rest of the way home.

✧◈◇━━◇━━◇◈✧

✦ To read a fact file on religious extremism, turn to page 309, then go to page 64 to continue with the story.

✦ To continue with the story now, go to page 64.

ahama wouldn't have wanted me to give away the pen, you think uneasily.

But then a firmer voice in your mind says: *She would have wanted you to stay* alive – *and this is a way you can do that.*

You bring the pen out of your pocket, and White Beard watches without a word as you unscrew it to reveal the memory stick.

You glance at his face. There's a light behind his eyes, and a pleased smile plays about his lips, as if he suspected you might have something like this and can only just restrain himself from grabbing it out of your hand.

'This is the only copy of the interview with Zayd,' you say. 'I'll give it to you in exchange for my freedom.'

'Well…' White Beard seems almost amused now. 'What a treasure. We were indeed hoping that you might be able to give us something like this. And of course it is worth your freedom…*if* it contains what you say it does. I'll have to take it from you to check.'

He holds his hand out for the pen, and you start to question whether you've done the right thing.

If I refuse to give it to him, though, you think, *won't he just take it by force?*

You're starting to feel a little foolish. But he did say it was worth your freedom. You have to hope that this deal will go through. So you hand him the pen.

He leaves the room, and you spend ten, then twenty, then thirty minutes chewing your fingernails. Just when you think it's a lost cause, White Beard comes back.

'Very good,' he says. 'That story was exactly what we needed. Now, your little sister must be worried about you – you'd better be getting along home.'

He holds the door to your room wide open.

'Really?' you ask disbelievingly.

'Oh, yes. I'm sorry to have kept you. Off you go.'

You walk out of the room, full of nerves, a flood of hope rising inside you. From the hallway, you see the two men who kidnapped you, one either side of the doorway. The door is wide open, but the expressions on the men's faces do not look kind. There is a dreadful curdling feeling in the pit of your stomach.

Run! shouts the voice in your mind, and you

begin to sprint for the open doorway. But the two men tackle you, bringing you crashing to the ground, and White Beard steps over you and slams the door closed. The two men begin to punch you, as White Beard stands over you and gives you a lecture.

'You do not bargain with al-Shabaab. You are not smarter than al-Shabaab. You do not leave al-Shabaab. The only thing you can give that al-Shabaab wants is your faith and your undying loyalty. You do not play games with al-Shabaab. You train, and if you are lucky, you will die a glorious soldier's death. Your life now is for jihad. Nothing else.

'Send him back to his room,' he commands, and the hail of blows stops. You struggle to get up, but Sunglasses drags you down the hallway by your ankle and throws you back into the same room as before. The door slams shut behind you.

FROM THAT POINT on, you try to escape so often that your nickname becomes Jiir Weyn: 'Rat'.

You try to escape from the locked room that night, and from the van the next day, when they take you to the desert for training. You make countless further attempts over the months you spend training in the desert, even though each ends in a beating.

You vow that you will never stop trying to get back to Jamilah. Your rage towards al-Shabaab – for taking your aunty from you, your sister, your home, your freedom – burns brighter with every passing setting of the sun.

Eventually, you decide the only way to escape is to lull al-Shabaab into a false sense of security, so you pretend to become a model recruit until, at last, your unit commander selects you to go on patrol in Mogadishu.

Your heart swells with hope as you approach your old neighbourhood. But when you arrive in your old street, where the grocery shop and your home once stood there is now nothing but charred rubble. There is no trace of Jamilah.

Your limbs stop working. Your heart, your body, your lungs – everything feels as heavy as wet concrete. The other boys in your patrol shout at you to move, but their voices seem to be coming from another planet. Only when an AMISOM solider starts running towards you, his weapon raised, does the adrenaline take over, and you run and hide just in time.

Something in you stops bouncing back that day. Instead, you become mute, obedient, filled with aggression. You stop crying, or looking at the stars at night in wonderment. You are no longer a child. There is something hollow in your heart, which al-Shabaab fills up with war.

The boys who fight beside you say they're your brothers, but when they die, you feel nothing – just a bricked-up deadness. It will be your turn to die one day, and you will welcome it.

For now, the only feeling you have left is a glimmer of pride when you see the fear in people's eyes as you walk towards them.

THE END

✳ To return to your last choice and try again, go to page 41.

You step back from the bomb and run across the street. You can still see the back of Rahama's red hijab through the window.

'*Bomb!*' you yell at the top of your lungs. '*Rahama, get out of the building!*'

Come on, come on, you think desperately, your heart hammering. Her head doesn't turn. She must be wearing her headphones. *Allah, help me now,* you pray.

'*Bomb!*' you shout again, and some people eye you warily; a few edge away from the building, unsure if they should believe you.

There's a small, broken piece of concrete at your feet. You pick it up and pelt it at Rahama's window, but you miss. The concrete falls onto the roof of an expensive-looking car parked nearby. The car alarm starts honking and wailing.

Good! you think, and you throw another rock at the window. This one clinks against the windowpane, then tumbles to the street and nearly hits a woman in a blue dress. She screams and looks around, outraged.

Any minute that bomb's going to go off, and right now I'm still close enough to be killed by it, you think.

'Come on, Rahama, come on! *Bomb!*' you yell again, so loudly that you feel a scraping in your throat.

Now people are taking notice. Some are muttering and walking away quickly. Others are shaking their heads and pointing at you.

'Hey!' shouts the woman in the blue dress, crossing the street. 'Did you just throw a rock?'

'Yes, because there's a—' you begin, but you're cut short by a shopkeeper.

'You hit my customer's car with your rock, you dumb kid! Didn't anyone ever teach you not to throw rocks?'

There's nothing for it. If you stay around to argue the reasons with them, the bomb will go off, and you'll all be killed. If you run, they might chase you. Maybe you can cause enough commotion on the street that Rahama will hear it, take notice and come outside too. Gulping back your fear, you turn and start sprinting.

'Hey!' shouts the shopkeeper.

'Stop that kid!' yells the woman.

You dart away down the street and cross the

road, dodging in front of cars and a goat-herder, your heart beating wildly in your chest. Someone swerves and falls off his bicycle. There is bleating and tooting and shouting.

The more noise the better, you think grimly.

'Idiot!'

'Stop!'

'What the hell are you doing?'

Angry faces surround you. Instead of helping the man on his bicycle up, on impulse you grab the fallen bike, and try to ride away.

A woman catches you, though. She gets you in a headlock, and is she ever strong. She must have raised twenty children, as she knows exactly how to put an end to mischief. 'A bike thief!' she shouts triumphantly.

'A rock-thrower! A vandal!' adds the shopkeeper.

'He won't pay for the damage he's caused. Teach him a lesson!' cries the bike-rider.

Any second now, you think. You pray desperately that Rahama is getting out. The woman forces your face-downwards onto the ground and you can hardly breathe. Spit and tears stream from your eyes and nose. You brace yourself, because you know the crowd is about to start raining blows on you.

'Criminal kids like these,' says the headlock woman

conversationally to the crowd, 'hah, I've caught dozens of them. They have no fathers to teach them morals. One day, Somalia will have a proper police force and strong families again. Until then, you just have to discipline them as best you can.'

With these words, the mob comes at you from all directions. You can't escape, and the blows become faster, until you're feeling scared you might black out. You pray for it to end soon.

'Stop!' shouts a commanding male voice. 'I know this boy. I will take responsibility for him.'

You struggle to look up and you see – to your horror – Qasim. His eyes have a hard, glittery look to them. The woman lets you go and you stand up slowly, massaging your neck. Everyone in the crowd takes a step back, like a pack of jackals when a lion steps into their midst.

'He is Rahama Daahir's nephew. I know where he lives. I'll take him home myself and see to it that this won't happen again.' When the crowd still seems wary, Qasim opens his wallet and starts handing out notes. 'For your troubles, madam. Please, sir, this will pay for your car's broken window.'

The crowd is pleased now: in their eyes, you have paid for the damage you caused and justice has been done. Qasim clasps your shoulder. Then he gets out his phone. Your heart stops. If he calls the number of the phone that's attached to the bomb, it will explode and Aunty Rahama will be killed.

'It's all right,' he tells you quietly in your ear. 'Walk away with me now, and you will come to no harm.'

You could walk away with Qasim. He has helped you to get away from the angry crowd, and perhaps it's safer to play along. Given that he could detonate the bomb at any moment, it seems unwise to enrage him, especially with the crowd on his side.

But you also know that Qasim is completely untrustworthy. You put your hand into your pocket and your fingers curl around a small weapon: Aunty Rahama's pen. Instead of playing along, you could stab him with its sharp nib, make a grab for his phone, and run.

What should you do?

✳ If you walk away with Qasim, go to page 61.
✳ If you try to fight Qasim, go to page 57.

You whip the pen out of your pocket. You stab it, as hard and fast as you can, towards Qasim's face, but he puts up his hand to block you. Your arms collide, and Qasim's phone falls to the ground. You both make a grab for it – but as Qasim bends over, you shove him, hard, and he loses balance. He sprawls on the pavement, and you grab the phone, pen still in your other hand, and start running.

Three strong-looking bearded men in black run towards you.

'He's Rahama Daahir's nephew!' you hear Qasim shout to them. 'He has the phone!'

You know that the men will do anything to get hold of Qasim's phone, and quickly, so that they can still detonate the bomb. They're not shooting just yet – probably because they don't want to raise the alarm and have people start to evacuate the area – but they might fire at you at any moment.

You see a broken hole in the pavement. A deep pool of dark-brown sewage sits below. You throw the phone down the hole, shove the pen in your pocket, and keep running.

'We'll get him – you finish the job!' you hear one of the men behind you shout.

You glance back and see Qasim peel off and begin to run away from you, towards the broadcast building. You duck and weave down the busy street, trying to shake off the three men still in hot pursuit. Every so often, you manage to glance behind you. An AMISOM soldier is running towards Qasim, and Qasim raises his gun, but he doesn't shoot the soldier. Instead, he points his gun at the backpack by the rubbish bin. He shoots the bomb.

A fountain of fire shoots upwards. The noise seems to rip the world in two.

Rahama.

An invisible wave of pressure slams your body and knocks you off your feet. There is a deafening crunch as the broadcast building collapses behind you. Smoke, ash and debris are falling all over the street, and the air is filled with screams. You struggle to your knees, then a piece of flying rubble hits the side of your head and you black out.

You wake up some hours later, as the sun is setting. AMISOM soldiers are pulling the debris away from around you.

'This kid's alive!' you hear one of them shout.

You sit up and brush off the dust and ash. Your whole body feels unsteady, as if there's a pile of scrambled eggs where your guts should be, but you're otherwise not badly hurt.

'Rahama?' you croak. 'She was in the broadcast building...'

Your rescuers' faces look grim.

'You're the only person we've found alive so far, this close to the blast,' one of them says, shaking his head sadly.

You manage to climb to your feet.

'Where are you going?' cries the soldier. 'Wait here and we'll take you to hospital!'

But you have to get back to Jamilah as soon as possible. You stumble away from the chaos, your breath coming in ragged gasps. You make it along street after street as night falls. When you see your street, relief washes over you. Safe at last.

Except, you realise suddenly, home isn't safe any longer. You still have a copy of the story that al-Shabaab killed Aunty Rahama for, hidden in your pocket. You were found at the bombsite trying to raise a distraction to foil their plans. You threw the detonator into the sewer, and that forced Qasim to shoot the bomb, which probably killed him, so you are partly responsible for Qasim's death now, too.

The men who were pursuing you knew you were Rahama's nephew – and even if they were killed, there's a good chance that more of them know where you live. You can only hope and pray that you get to Jamilah before they do.

✳ To read a fact file on religious extremism, turn to page 309, then go to page 64 to continue with the story.

✳ To continue with the story now, go to page 64.

You let Aunty Rahama's pen fall back into your pocket. You walk away from the crowd, Qasim's hand firmly on your shoulder.

'Um...thank you, Qasim,' you say, acting like this is just a normal situation and you don't know anything about the bomb. 'I, uh, promise I won't get up to any more mischief...'

'That's right. You won't.' Qasim's voice is as hard as his hand. He is steering you towards the broadcast building. You are still a safe distance away from it, but you are facing it now.

Qasim moves his grip from your shoulder down to your hand. 'I want you to see what happens to those who ignore Allah's law; who disrespect al-Shabaab.'

With his free hand, he holds the phone in front of you. You see a number on the screen. With his other hand, the one holding yours, he forces your finger towards the green 'call' button.

'Call this number,' Qasim says. 'Call it, and you will see what we are capable of.'

'Go to hell!' you shout, and with all your strength you try to wrestle away from him. But Qasim is much stronger than you are; he won't release your hand. You panic.

'*Bomb! Bomb!*' you start screaming. 'There's a bomb in the broadcast building! He's trying to make me blow it up! *Bomb!*'

Qasim's eyes light up with fury. You manage to snatch the phone from his other hand, and you smash it against the ground with all your might. Qasim growls like an enraged dog and grabs you around your neck. You feel his fingers pressing into your throat.

'That was a stupid thing you just did,' he hisses.

Another bearded man in black – an al-Shabaab militant – appears at Qasim's side. 'People are starting to notice!' he snaps. 'Why haven't you detonated it?'

Qasim stiffens to attention. This man seems to be his superior. 'This boy just destroyed the detonator,' he mumbles, nodding towards the broken phone at your feet, and for a hopeful moment you think you've foiled their plan.

But the other man presses a gun into Qasim's hand. 'Then go and finish it yourself,' he barks. 'I'll take care of the boy!'

Qasim runs towards the broadcast building with the gun in his hand. You break free of the other man's grip and start sprinting after him, shouting, 'Stop that man! There's a bomb!'

People are screaming and running away now. Qasim glances back at you and raises his gun.

You think, *Allah, please, help me.*

But instead of shooting you, Qasim turns again, points his gun at the black backpack...and shoots the bomb.

You are hurtling through the air. There is no up or down anymore, only the blast, and you are inside it. The noise rips through you. You are caught in a cartwheel of debris and death.

Time slows, and though even the air itself seems to be on fire, a calm and thoughtful voice in your head simply says: *So, this is how I die.*

A huge piece of concrete topples from the broadcast building. You see it falling towards you. Your last thought is just: *Jamilah.* Then you are slammed to the ground. The impact kills you instantly.

Rahama's golden pen melts in the fire, taking her story with it – now just another mystery held in Allah's unknowable hand.

THE END

✳ To return to your last choice and try again, go to page 56.

You creep down the alleyway to the back door of your home. You can hear a whimpering, like the sound of a puppy who's been left alone in the dark. You open the door a crack and the whimpering stops. You can't push the door open any further, because someone is huddled against it, trying to keep it closed.

'Jamilah,' you call softly, 'it's okay. It's me. Let me in.'

The door swings open and Jamilah gives in to sobs. 'I hate you!' she shouts. 'I *hate* you!' But she's clinging to you like she's drowning.

'It's okay. I'm sorry you were all alone…'

'I heard a bomb!' She hiccups. Her shoulders are shaking. 'And then you didn't come back, for hours and hours. Where *were* you?'

You take in a sharp breath. This quivering, messy, terrified child is yours now. Nobody else is going to protect her, or explain to her what's happened. Whether she lives or dies could well come down to the choices you will make in the days and weeks to come.

Now you know how Aunty Rahama must have felt, when she was left to raise you both after al-Shabaab laid siege to the marketplace where your hooyo and aabe worked and they were killed. You want someone bigger and wiser than you, showing the way. But you're it.

There's a note, you remember. *She said to look under her pillow. She said it will explain everything.*

'Where's Aunty Rahama?' Jamilah asks you. 'Where *is* she?'

You can't answer her – not yet. You pull Jamilah down to sit with you on Rahama's bed, keeping her close with one arm while reaching for Rahama's pillow with the other. It still smells like her. You blink away hot tears.

Under Rahama's pillow, your fingers find a piece of folded paper. You can only pray that this letter will hold a clue as to what you should do next. You don't want Jamilah to see how scared you are.

As you unfold the letter, a wad of banknotes falls out, and you quickly stash it in your pocket with the pen. You breathe a sigh of gratitude. Now at least you'll have a little cash to help you.

To my favourite nephew (all right, you're my only nephew),

When I was little, I found an ants' nest in the corner of our food cupboard. I poked it with a stick, and the ants came for me. I squashed as many as I could, but there were too many, and I was badly bitten. Writing reports exposing the truth about al-Shabaab has had the same effect.

If you're reading this, it probably means that al-Shabaab has finally caught up with me. But please try not to be sad. Instead, be fast, be smart, be brave. When your mum and dad were killed and you came to me, I was only two years older than you are now. I know you can do everything I did, and more.

Keep out of al-Shabaab's way. They don't know that you and Jamilah exist, or about the pen and what it contains.

That pen is my sword! It was a gift from a man I love, an Australian–Somali called Aadan Williams. I'm sorry I haven't told you about him sooner – he lives in Melbourne, Australia, and I've been looking for a way for us to move there too, but it was too early to get your hopes up. He is a journalist like me, so he understands why I've risked my life for the truth.

If something bad does happen to me, I want you to call Aadan on the Australian number on the back of this letter. Tell him what's happened, and he should be able to help you.

This pen really means so much to me. In the darkest of times, it's given me hope that freedom does exist.

Now I pass it on to you, because there is no one else I know in the world with such an enquiring mind and fearless heart. You are a special boy. I haven't managed yet to work out what Cross the river on the banner of the eagle *means, or to find out anything more about Bright Dream. Take this pen, and with Aadan's help, finish what I couldn't.*

I love you. Look after Jamilah for me, and tell her I love her too.

Aunty Rahama

Through your tears, you flip the letter over and see Aadan's phone number on the back. You hope fervently that Aunty Rahama was right – that Aadan will be able to help you. The money now in your pocket won't last you more than a few weeks.

Rahama was wrong about one thing, though: al-Shabaab certainly *do* know that you and Jamilah exist, probably thanks to Qasim – and they're likely coming to find you right now.

Jamilah is shaking, still clinging to you. Her hair is damp with sweat.

'I don't want you to leave me alone ever again,' she says accusingly. 'We have to stay here together and wait for Aunty Rahama to come home.'

She has no idea how much danger you're truly in. And she's so frightened and so young. How can you make her understand? How can you tell her that Rahama is dead?

You take a deep, shaky breath. 'Jamilah,' you say, stroking her damp hair, 'Aunty Rahama's not coming home. I'm so sorry.'

'No,' says Jamilah, starting to cry. 'You're lying!'

You cup her chin in your hand and make her look at you. 'I know you don't want to believe me, but it's true,' you insist. 'The bad guys from Arsenal found her, and we have to go, before they come and find us too.'

Jamilah buries her face in your chest and begins to sob in earnest. You want to hold her and comfort her, but instead you pull her to her feet.

'Come on,' you say firmly. 'We have to go *now*.'

Jamilah's eyes are huge. 'Go where?' she asks.

She has a point. You don't know. 'Anywhere safe,' you say. 'We need to pack – quickly. And then I need to find a phone.'

You hear the roar of an approaching engine, which stops right outside your home, then a sliding door opening and closing. You freeze, and Jamilah wraps her arms around you.

'Quick, go!' you hiss and push her off you.

There is a metallic rattle as someone tries to lift the locked roller door at the front of the grocery shop.

Grabbing Jamilah's hand, you escape through the back door into the alleyway. You hear footsteps approaching.

'We'll kill them if we have to,' a voice mutters. 'But the main thing is to bring back that golden pen.'

You sprint in the other direction, pulling Jamilah with you so hard that she runs with stumbling, flying feet. You squeeze between two houses, jump a ditch, and then you're out on the road. You keep running until you're halfway to Lido Beach.

You stop running, gasping for breath, and wonder if it would be safe to go and hide in the ruin with the lime lady for the rest of the night.

And then the bottom seems to fall out of your stomach, like fruit through a wet paper bag.

'The letter!' you cry to Jamilah. You see it in your mind's eye, falling to the floor as Jamilah cried in your arms. You left it – and Aadan Williams' phone number – behind. That number was a lifeline to Australia. You try desperately to remember it, but it's no good – you only glanced at it, you didn't memorise it.

'I need that number!' you hiss. You feel like screaming. Your fists are clenched into balls. How could you have been so dumb? Maybe Rahama was wrong to believe that you could do this.

Steady on, says a voice in your ear. You know it's just your imagination, but it feels like Rahama is talking to you. *You and Jamilah got out of there alive – you're doing so well. You'll find a way through this.*

You reach into your pocket to touch the pen and the money, and try to calm your mind down. *Think.*

Al-Shabaab will search the house and take anything valuable or interesting to them. They might even set fire to what's left.

You could spend the night in the ruins, and go back to look for the letter in the morning, but you'll be lucky if it isn't gone by then. Or you could run back now, without Jamilah, and take your chances trying to steal the letter from under al-Shabaab's noses.

The clouds shift and the moonlight silvers the tears in Jamilah's eyes. 'What now?' she whispers.

✳ If you run back to the house for the letter now, go to page 71.

✳ If you decide to spend the night in the ruins and look for the letter in the morning, go to page 74.

'I have to go back and get that letter,' you tell Jamilah. 'It included the phone number of a man in Australia who can help us. If I don't go back now, it won't be there in the morning.'

You pray you're not already too late.

You'd like to take Jamilah to the lime lady, but there's no time. Instead, you leave her hiding behind a pile of rubbish by a building, telling her not to move. Then you run for home.

You stop in the alleyway, metres from your doorway. You can hear voices inside.

'There's nothing here of use,' curses one voice. 'We've searched everything. Torch the place.'

'Wait!' says another voice. 'What's that piece of paper under the bed there? See – there?'

There's a brief pause, and a rustle. 'A letter!' says the first voice. He lets out a brief, sarcastic laugh. 'Aunty was saying goodbye to her darlings...'

Your heart sinks. Now you will have to steal the letter from their very hands. How can you possibly achieve that? You hear a sloshing sound and smell petrol. *Oh, no.* They're preparing to burn your home to the ground.

'Careful, you idiot! You nearly got it on me,' snaps the first voice.

'Get out of the way then,' replies the second in a surly tone, 'and let's go and find the kids.'

Now's your chance – while they're distracted arguing with each other.

You charge into the room, towards the man with the petrol can. You shove him, and he is doused in petrol. Some splashes onto you too, feeling oily against your skin. The fumes make your head spin.

As the man with the petrol can fumbles and swears, you leap at the other man and snatch at the letter.

'Oh, so this is important, is it?' he sneers, holding it up high like a meaty bone in front of a dog. 'So important you came back and risked your life— *Ow!*'

He stops mid-sentence as you give him a hefty kick in the crotch and make another snatch for the letter while he's doubled over.

The letter is now in your hands, but the petrol man crash-tackles you from behind. You roll together on the fuel-soaked floor. Some gets in your mouth; it tastes bitter and awful. The other man leans down and snatches the letter from your fingertips. At the same moment, you see a cigarette lighter tumble from the petrol man's pocket onto the floor beside you.

You grab the lighter and brandish it wildly. 'Stop!' you shout. 'Give me that letter and let me go, or we'll all burn!'

The man you were fighting – who is even more petrol-soaked than you are – looks worried, but the other man, standing over you both, merely smiles. He folds up the letter and slips it into his pocket. When his hand comes out of his pocket, you see that he, too, is holding a lighter.

'Two can play at that game,' he says. And before your mind can even really process what's happening – and without any attempt to help save his petrol-soaked friend on the floor – he leaps for the door, reaches back inside, and holds his lighter up to the orange curtain over the window.

Woomph. The curtain bursts into flame. The petrol-soaked man gives an enraged yell and throws himself at the door too, but he doesn't make it – now he is a screaming tornado of flame.

The rest of the room is alight within milliseconds, and you are swallowed by the flames.

THE END

✦ To return to your last choice and try again, go to page 70.

You sigh. You've narrowly escaped from al-Shabaab twice now. To go back and try your luck a third time would be madness. Maybe they'll overlook the letter. It's just a piece of paper on the ground. It'll still be there in the morning.

While you hold Jamilah's hand and walk to the ruined theatre by the sea, you entertain a brief fantasy: you will go back tomorrow; the house will be untouched; and you will call Aadan and he will say, *Please, call me uncle!* and immediately send you two tickets to Australia.

The little hovel in the ruin is deserted. You wonder what happened to the lime lady. You show Jamilah to the hole in the floor where you hid with Zayd and Rahama, and you huddle there together silently in the dusty dark. Then waves of sleep crash and recede as you lie there, exhausted and on guard, half-awake the whole night.

Fragments of plans drift through your brain. If you can't contact Aadan, you could hide here in the ruin until al-Shabaab stops looking for you. How long would that take? Would your few weeks' worth of money get you through? What would happen if they *did* find you? If they found Jamilah...

Or you could go to the countryside, where you might find some people of the same clan as you who would take you in. But the whole country is in the grip of a fierce drought, so there won't be much spare food to go round. Besides, al-Shabaab controls a lot of the countryside – so the chances of you being caught there are even higher.

Or you could try to get across the border, into Ethiopia or Kenya. It wouldn't be easy, and you'd have to spend almost all your money getting there – and al-Shabaab does have a presence there too – but at least those countries are at peace.

When dawn comes, it's a relief to be released from the endless circling of your thoughts, and instead to begin to take action. The lime lady left behind a little kettle of water, and you and Jamilah use it to wash, then you kneel on cardboard boxes for your morning prayer.

Your prayer mat at home belonged to your father. It has three worn patches in the places where he pressed his forehead and knees, five times every day, till the day he died. If it's still there when you go home, it will be the one sentimental treasure you will bring with you on your journey. You make Jamilah wait in the ruins while you slip back towards your place.

You hear the yelling before you can see the source. It's the deep, booming voice of Mr Jabril, the grocery shop owner and your landlord.

'Why me?' he is wailing. 'All my savings, my family's livelihood, gone!'

The word 'gone' hits your chest like a stone. *Please no, please no…*

You come into sight of the place you used to live: it's now a smoking, charred wreck. Neighbours' houses and shops are damaged too, and the neighbours stand in the street, pointing fingers, laying blame for the damage and haggling over who will pay. An AMISOM guard walks by, looking over the commotion.

'It must have been your tenants! They should pay!' cries the hairdresser from across the road.

'They probably died in the fire,' sobs Mr Jabril. 'Those poor children…' He shakes his head helplessly.

You think about running to him. But you don't want a dozen angry neighbours turning on you. If you get the blame for this fire, you might have to give them all the money in your pocket just to appease them and get away.

That's it, then – your lifeline to Australia is gone.

So is your prayer mat, Jamilah's teddy – everything. Your only hope now is that there might be some information on the pen, or even just on the internet, that will help you track Aadan down. But for that, you'll need a computer.

By the time you get back to the ruin, you've decided: you're going to spend the money trying to get to Kenya's capital, Nairobi. Kenya's the closest country to Mogadishu, and you've heard hundreds of Somalis cross the border every year, escaping the war and the famine.

You take Jamilah's hand and look around the little hide-out. On impulse, you pick up a stick and scratch your initials into the dirt – you don't want to leave your home town without somehow saying *I was here* – but then you think better of it and rub out every trace. Instead, you just write the word 'goodbye'. Then you wrap your arm around Jamilah's shoulders and begin the walk to the marketplace.

BY ASKING A few questions in the marketplace, you find out that there is one man, a carpet-seller, who also does business in Kenya. You see a truck being loaded up with carpets, and you guess that the man in the blue shirt who seems to be giving the orders is the owner. You don't know how to go about asking this man if he'll do something illegal – take you and Jamilah across the border.

Eventually, you approach him and ask: 'Will you take a package to Kenya for me?'

'How big is this package?' he asks sceptically.

'Uh... about as big as me and my sister,' you reply. You take nearly all the notes from your pocket.

The man narrows his eyes and looks you up and down. He knows what you're *really* asking. 'Can you keep her quiet at the checkpoints?' he asks, nodding to Jamilah.

'I'm not stupid – I'll stay quiet,' she says defiantly.

'Huh,' says the man drily. 'Not stupid, eh? You could have fooled me. Look, it's not up to me to ask why you're doing this, but just know that if you get caught by soldiers or the police without identity papers, they can throw you straight back across the border. Happens to Somalis all the time. Half my business comes from taking them back there again. I'll do it, though.'

After the man has loaded his truck, he pushes you and Jamilah into a hiding place at the back of his truck among the dozens of rolls of carpet. As the door slams shut and the engine starts to rumble, Jamilah begins to cry.

'I don't like that man,' she whimpers. 'It was a bad idea to go with him. I think we should stay here in Somalia.'

'Shoosh, Jamilah,' you whisper.

The man's warning words are echoing in your head, but you choose to ignore them, telling yourself: *We'll figure it out when we get there.*

'If you're quiet, I'll let you see Aunty Rahama's story pen.'

'What do you mean, story pen?' asks Jamilah.

You and Rahama have always told stories to Jamilah before bed every night. Now you need a story to make Jamilah feel safe and brave. You take Aunty Rahama's pen from your pocket. The ruby twinkles in the dim light.

'You saw her give this to us after school,' you say, showing it to her. She nods, her eyes bright with wonder. 'It's a story pen – and story pens are magical. They don't need ink, because they run on love and laughter. When someone holds a story pen in their hands, they will think of a wonderful tale, and everyone else will listen. Are you ready for a story? All this carpet is reminding me of something that once happened to Igal Shidal.'

Jamilah chuckles. 'Igal Shidal is always so silly!' she says. 'I like those stories.'

'Well, you'll love this one,' you say. You feel warmth returning to your voice, as if Aunty Rahama were sitting right beside you with her arm around you.

It's dim and stuffy in the back of the truck. The engine rumbles and the truck sways as it makes its way through the morning traffic.

Goodbye, Mogadishu, you think to yourself. You don't know if you'll ever see your home city again.

You swallow the lump in your throat and say to Jamilah, 'Did I ever tell you about the time some bad men came after Igal Shidal? They wanted to kill him.'

'That doesn't sound funny,' says Jamilah worriedly.

'But Igal Shidal had a plan. He called his wife – he was always so bossy to his wife. He said, "Hey, wife! The bad men are coming! Hurry up! I'm going to pretend I'm already dead. Get a carpet and roll me up in it!"

'So his wife got a carpet and rolled up Igal Shidal. "Now drag me out onto the porch!" came his voice from inside the carpet. "Quickly, before they get here. Oh, you're so slow, woman!"

'Igal Shidal's wife dragged him out onto the porch all rolled up in his carpet. "I can hear them coming!" she whispered. "The bad men are on their way to this house! What shall I do?"

'"Get down on your knees, silly wife, and cry over the carpet, and say, *Oh, my poor husband Igal Shidal is dead!* They will believe you and leave us alone," he commanded.

'"Waah! Waah! Oh, my poor husband!" she cried. The men were approaching the house.

'"Cry louder!" said Igal Shidal from inside the carpet. "Is that all the crying you would do if I were *really* dead?" You see, he couldn't stop bossing his wife around even when he was pretending to be dead.

'The men came up the steps. The wife was wailing. Igal Shidal was all rolled up in the carpet.

'"Is your husband dead?" asked one of the men.

'"Yes, my poor husband, waah!"

'The man was suspicious. "Really? When did he die?"

'Then came Igal Shidal's voice, loud and clear from inside the carpet: "Say he died yesterday!"

'"He, um, he died yesterday," said the obedient wife, but too late, because everyone had heard Igal Shidal's voice from inside the carpet!

'The bad men unrolled him, and they said, "This man is pathetic. He is such a coward he pretended to be dead rather than face us, and he couldn't even pretend to be dead properly. Such an idiot is no threat to us! Let him live here with the women and children." And the bad men went on their way!'

Jamilah nuzzles into your arm as the truck sways along. '*Tell them I died yesterday!*' she chuckles quietly.

After a while, the sounds of the city die away, and the back of the van begins to heat up in the desert sun. The warmth, the darkness and the swaying soothe you both to sleep.

YOU WAKE A couple of hours later when the truck lurches to a sudden stop. You hear men's voices.

'Get down,' you say to Jamilah. 'This is a checkpoint, and Kenyan soldiers might want to check the truck. Get under the carpet and don't make a sound.'

'Not like Igal Shidal,' Jamilah whispers, and despite the horrible situation you're in, a tiny smile crosses your lips.

You wriggle down just in time: with a rolling, metallic roar, the back of the truck is opened, and light floods in.

You feel the truck bounce as the soldiers jump up into it to search it, and then: *Thump. Thump.* They are hitting and kicking at the carpets, and getting closer and closer to where you are lying!

One of them kicks the carpet you're under. The carpet muffles the blow, so it doesn't hurt, but you have to fight hard not to cry out in surprise. You desperately need to cough. You try to swallow and force away the clawing itch in your throat.

'Unroll these carpets,' you hear a soldier's voice command.

'What, all of them?' says the truck driver's voice. He must be inside the truck too as he sounds close. 'I can unroll one or two, sir, but to do them all would take—'

'Shut up and do it or you'll be arrested!'

You feel your carpet move as the driver grabs the carpet nearest to you. You hear a hiss as it is dragged from the van, and the flapping sound of it being unrolled. You can also hear your heart booming like a hip-hop anthem. You're still trying desperately not to cough.

The truck driver speaks again, his voice low and persuasive this time: 'Sir, I know that if I were to deliver this consignment on time, my customers would be so happy they would pay extra. Is there a way to fast-track this?'

He's offering the soldier a bribe to let you through without unrolling any more carpets! It works. There is some muttering, the door slams shut, and you're on your way again.

You whisper thanks to Allah under your breath: '*Alhamd lilah*!'

Two hours later, you almost wish that the soldiers would search the truck again just to give you some air. This metal box you're in is now as hot as an oven. Jamilah's head rolls around on her neck. Her eyes are glazed, and her lips form little raised squares of dry skin. Your own tongue feels like a bloated, dry sponge in your mouth. You give Jamilah sips of the water the driver gave you. It's now as warm as a cup of tea.

Finally, after what feels like another two hours, the driver stops, in the middle of the desert. The air that rushes into the back when he opens the door is hot and dry, but at least it's fresh. Relieved, you climb out into the searing afternoon sunlight. The road ripples like oil in a blue-hazed heat mirage. Enormous salt pans glitter, and sandy wind stings your skin. A tough, black thorn tree is the only sign of life.

The driver refills your water bottle from a blue plastic drum he keeps in the front of the truck.

'Do a wee if you need to,' he says gruffly, but you and Jamilah shake your heads – you're both so dehydrated that you don't need to. 'We'll stop for the night at Garissa. You two will need to stay in the truck.'

He gives you some water to wash yourselves before you all begin the Asr prayer. Your croaky voices reciting the words, and the buzzing of the flies seeking out moisture in the corners of your mouth and eyes, are the only sounds.

You set off again. The truck slowly cools as the sun gets lower. You eat some flatbread the driver gave you earlier for dinner, and slowly the cracks and pin-pricks of light in the back of the truck dim to black.

You wake briefly when the truck comes to a standstill at Garissa and the driver takes his rest. In the morning the truck's engine starts again, and by late afternoon you can hear the honking and hubbub of a big city.

The truck pulls to a stop and the driver opens the door and helps you and Jamilah out. Your legs feel shaky. The truck's parked in a large vacant garage, which seems to be below ground. There is nobody else in sight.

'We're in Eastleigh, a suburb of Nairobi,' the driver tells you. 'This is where all the Somalis in Kenya live, except the ones in the camps.'

You have to pay the driver extra to cover the bribe he gave at the checkpoint, which leaves you with only two five-hundred-shilling notes left – enough for one or two days' food. You feel sick handing over the money, but he saved your life, so you thank him. Then you walk up the garage's steep entry ramp and out onto the street.

You hold hands with Jamilah as you walk along the sealed road, both of you wide-eyed. Mogadishu is a big city, but it's nothing like modern, over-developed Nairobi. Skyscrapers tower above you. A rubbish truck with sweeper-brooms rumbles past, making you jump. A woman chatters in Swahili on a mobile phone, shopping bags over her arm, her hair exposed and shining in the afternoon light.

You lead Jamilah into a grocery shop. A bell beeps and cold air blasts your head as you walk through the door. When you try to buy two bananas, the shopkeeper points you to a money-changer down the road.

You swap your remaining thousand Somali shillings for three crisp Kenyan notes: a hundred, a fifty, and a twenty. You blink, hoping that these Kenyan shillings can buy much more than a Somali shilling does at home. The notes are brown, yellow and blue, with a bearded, baggy-eyed man printed on them.

You return to the grocery shop to buy the two

bananas. The shopkeeper takes your twenty-shilling note, and he doesn't give you any change.

You and Jamilah then wander down the street until you see a beautiful green park. Looking around tentatively, you find a bench and sit down to eat.

A Kenyan man in a suit walks past. A dog with a rope on its neck walks beside him, and you stare curiously. Won't the dog bite him?

'What are you looking at, refugee scum?' the man mutters in English as he passes you. 'Nick off back to Somalia, filthy kids.' His dog snarls.

Jamilah tucks her feet up under her on the bench. You clench your jaw and squeeze her hand.

'Don't worry. Not everyone here will be like that,' you say to her.

You need a plan for how to survive. Your money might be nearly gone, but Aunty Rahama also left you the pen. What if there's some extra information on there that would help – like another copy of Aadan's number in Australia?

You take the pen out of your pocket and unscrew it to examine the memory stick hidden inside. You could break the memory stick out of the pen and sell the rest, but it's too beautiful, it meant too much to Aunty Rahama, and you wouldn't want to risk breaking the memory stick itself. The pen's ruby glints in the sunlight.

You still haven't told Jamilah everything – not about the interview with Zayd, or what really happened after Aunty Rahama gave you the pen, while Jamilah was waiting at home scared out of her wits. But she's been so brave on this trip, and you're in this together now. You decide she's old enough to know the truth. But before you can begin—

'Hey,' says another man walking by, 'what's that you have?' He's speaking Somali, but with a strange accent. He has a pot belly and is wearing a white shirt with lots of chest hair poking out of its neck.

'Nothing,' you reply quickly, but he comes closer, suspicious.

You quickly slip the pen away into your pocket, cursing yourself for having brought it out in public.

'That looked like a valuable pen,' says the man. 'Since when do young kids have something like that?'

'He thinks we stole it!' whispers Jamilah urgently.

The man is right on top of you now. 'Give it to me!' he demands. 'We need to hand that over to the police. Come on, now.'

'This is *our* pen! Go away!' shouts Jamilah, and then, to your horror, she pulls a horrible face at the man.

You slap Jamilah's knee and shoosh her. You know from the truck driver that if you get into any sort of trouble in Kenya, you could be thrown out of the country by the police for having no identity papers.

You glance around. You and Jamilah can probably run faster than this overweight man, so if you start running now maybe you'll have a good chance of getting away.

On the other hand, if you tell him the truth about why you have the pen, he might just believe you – though it is an incredible story.

What will you do?

✳ If you run away from the man, go to page 101.

✳ If you tell the man your story, go to page 90

✳ To read a fact file on crossing borders 'illegally', turn to page 311, then return to this page to make your choice.

You take a deep breath and prepare to tell the man your story. But to your amazement, he starts laughing at Jamilah.

'That *face*!' he chuckles. 'Goodness me, child, that was uglier than a monkey's butt!'

You laugh too. 'I'm sorry about my little sister,' you apologise. 'She can be very…naughty.'

'That's all right,' says the man. 'So, you say it's your pen, huh? I find that hard to believe. Why are you sitting on a park bench looking like a pair of unwashed monkeys if you have something as valuable as that in your possession?'

You like this man straight away. He tells you his name is Sampson. His fat belly shakes when he laughs – and he laughs a lot.

Your story pours out of you: how you came to have the pen; how you came to Kenya. What happened to Aunty Rahama. Jamilah listens wide-eyed, adding in the bits she knows. It's such a relief to have a kind adult to speak to.

When you're done, Sampson says: 'Come and walk with me. I have a shop with better food than those overpriced bananas.'

Sampson's shop is at the base of a tall apartment block.

'It's all Somalis living here,' he tells you, gesturing to the enormous building. 'I was raised a Christian, then I fell in love with my wife, a Somali Muslim, so now do you know what I call myself? I'm a *Chris–Mus*!'

You want to tell Sampson that's not right, that he can't be both at once, but he is laughing too hard at his own joke for you to speak over the top of him.

'Chris–Mus, get it? Like the holiday!' He wipes away tears as he takes out his key, removes the 'Back in 5 minutes' sign from the door, and leads you inside his shop.

You look around. There are bags of rice, and boxes of biscuits, tuna and hot sauce. There's a yellow desk with posters stuck to the front of it advertising international calling cards, and on top of the desk, next to the register, is a large grey computer.

You have a bold idea. 'Mr Sampson, sir?' you ask.

'Just Sampson is fine, my dear boy.'

'My sister and I used to live behind a grocery shop in Mogadishu, and we're used to helping out. We would be happy to sweep your floors and unpack your boxes, or anything you'd like, if...'

'Come on, out with it! You want a place to stay? No worries! Just ask!'

You gulp. Sampson's generosity is amazing. 'Actually, I wanted to know if we could use your computer, to read what's on the pen's memory stick.'

'And we want a place to stay, too!' cries Jamilah joyfully.

You pinch her. In your culture, it's more polite to refuse at first, so as not to seem overeager or greedy. But Sampson just laughs.

'All right, my little flower. Just don't pull that monkey-butt face at me again, okay? Aiieee! I thought my face would crack off just from looking at it!'

He grabs his face in mock pain. Jamilah laughs until she is gasping for breath. Her laughter is the best sound in the world.

For the last few hours of the day, you and Jamilah work hard in Sampson's busy shop. You want to prove that you are worthy of the trust he's put in you.

That evening, after all the customers have left, Sampson locks the door and flips the 'Open' sign over to 'Closed', and you plug the pen into his computer. Sampson and Jamilah crowd around you.

The computer whirs, clunks and hums. Your fingernails are digging into your palms.

Please let Aadan's number be on here, as well as

the interview with Zayd. Please let there be some clue about what to do next.

You gasp – there are three files on the memory stick! The first is, indeed, a sound recording of the interview with Zayd.

'Let's hear it!' Sampson cries. You're dying to find out what's in the other two files, but you want to be obliging to your host.

You, Jamilah and Sampson listen to the interview together. Hearing it all again takes you right back to the lime lady's ruin: the terror of hiding in that hole and hearing al-Shabaab drag Zayd away. Listening to Rahama's voice again is bittersweet. At the end of the interview, you wipe hot tears from your eyes. Jamilah lets out a loud sob, and you hug her close.

'Phew,' says Sampson. 'Now I know why Arsenal came after you. Your aunty was going to broadcast that? She's a hero.'

The second file is titled 'Bright Dream'. It's an email from Aadan to Aunty Rahama.

To: rahamadaahir@gmail.com
From: aadanwilliams@bigpond.net.au
    Dearest Rahama,
    I've started to look into Bright Dream (www.brightdream.org.sm). On the surface, they look like

a regular orphanage, raising funds for kids of war.

If they're doing something dodgy, it should show up in their bank account transaction history. Their donations form lists an account with Nile Bank, number 1793 2026. I haven't been able to guess their password, though.

Rahama, I'm so proud of what you're doing, and I know how much you care about your work, but it feels more and more urgent to me that you get out of Somalia. How is your visa application going? I dream of the day you and the kids will be here living in Australia with me.

All my love,

Aadan

The third file is a Word document called 'My Story'. But when you try to open it, a notice comes up: 'This file is password protected. Please enter your password.'

Why would Rahama have left a password-protected document on this pen and not told you what the password is? Did she expect you to guess? You try a few different words and names, but nothing unlocks the document.

My Story, you think. *Whose story is on there? What does it mean?* You sigh.

'What are you sighing for, boy?' asks Sampson.

'You have the email address of your aunty's boyfriend in Australia now. You can contact him that way.'

He's right! You were so busy reading the body of the email that you failed to notice Aadan's email address there at the top!

'Can you help me send an email?' you ask.

'Leave it to me,' says Sampson. 'We can use my email account. I can write tonight to tell him where you are, and let him know what's happened. You can use my phone to call him as soon as he replies to the email. Now, let's get you comfy for the night.'

Sampson makes a bed of blankets at the back of the shop for you both. 'I'm sorry I can't take you home,' he apologises. 'We have my wife's whole family visiting in our tiny apartment at the moment – you couldn't squeeze a mouse in there! I wish I could show you more hospitality. There's a saying in Swahili: *Kwenye ng'ombe kuna pembe* – where there are cows, there are horns. You take the good with the bad, hey?'

Once Sampson has left and you've completed your Isha'a prayer, Jamilah falls asleep straight away, but you lie awake listening to the hum of the shop's refrigerator and the rumble of passing cars. You hope that Aadan will reply soon with a number you can call him on. What could be hidden on the password-protected document? And how can you find out more about Bright Dream if you can't log in to their bank account?

Just as you're starting to drift off, two pieces of the puzzle click into place. Bright Dream's account is with *Nile* Bank – and the Nile is the most famous river in Africa. Zayd said: *Cross the river on the banner of the eagle.* What if 'the river' is Nile Bank? What if 'banner of the eagle', or something like it, is Bright Dream's internet banking password?

'Cross the river on the banner of the eagle,' you say eagerly to Sampson the next morning as soon as he walks in the door, then you explain your thinking.

Together, you, Sampson and Jamilah go to the Nile Bank log-in page online and try 'banneroftheeagle' as the password. No luck.

And there's been no email reply from Aadan yet – no luck there either.

'What *is* the banner of the eagle, anyway?' asks Sampson. He types the words into Google. His computer hums and whirrs again, then an image comes up in the search results.

Sampson gasps. 'The terrorist flag!'

You recognise the flag, but you never knew it was called 'the banner of the eagle'. It's a black flag covered in white Arabic calligraphy.

'It's not a terrorist flag – it's an old Muslim flag,' you say. 'It's been around for ages. It doesn't belong to Arsenal, but they've taken it and twisted it for their own use... just like everything else.'

'What does the writing on it say?' asks Sampson.

'It says: "There is no God but Allah, and Mohammed is his messenger." It's the Shahada – the Muslim declaration of faith.'

For a moment, you forget about the search for the password as you think of your mosque. These words – the Kalima Shahada – are written on the inside walls in beautiful calligraphy. As you close your eyes, you can almost smell the sweet, earthy smoke of the *uunsi* incense they burn there. You remember the voice of your imam, and your heart aches as you wonder if you'll ever find another mosque anywhere in the world just like it.

Sampson interrupts your thoughts. 'What if the password is "Shahada"?' he suggests.

'I don't think so,' you say. 'It would be too obvious – only someone pretty stupid would pick that.'

'Or someone who thinks they'll never be caught,' says Jamilah.

She has a point. You type in *Shahada*, and to your astonishment the page changes and a world of numbers opens up before your eyes. You're inside Bright Dream's bank account!

Your and Sampson's eyes goggle.

'Whoa,' breathes Sampson. 'That is *much* too much money for an orphanage to have.'

He's right. The numbers have so many zeros in them that you can't keep track, so you click 'Display in US dollars', and even then, it's still in the millions. There is some serious money moving in and out of this account.

'The orphans should all be driving Mercedes Benzes with that kind of money,' Sampson says.

'This is serious,' you say. 'This is proof of who they're buying their weapons from, and who's giving them funds.' You look down the page. 'By checking the dates and the places of each transaction, we can work out roughly where the leaders of Arsenal have been living and hiding all over Somalia!'

Sampson gasps. 'I shouldn't have done this,' he mutters. 'Quickly, log off!'

He closes the page, shuts down his computer, and looks about the room, terrified.

'I should have thought of that!' he wails. 'When you log on to a bank account from an unknown computer, the bank immediately sends a message to the account holder saying there's been a new log-in from an unknown source! What if Arsenal traces it back to me? They'll come and kill me!'

You didn't know that could happen. Jamilah gives a little whimper and squeezes Sampson tight. You try to think fast. You imagine that your brain is whirring and clunking just like Sampson's computer.

'Can you ask the police for protection?' you say. 'They'd be interested in knowing about Bright Dream.'

Sampson sighs and chews a fingernail. A customer comes into the shop, and he serves them.

'The problem with going to the police,' he says when he's finished, 'is that once they found out *you* are the source of the information about Bright Dream, they'd probably throw you out of the country. They're supposed to let you stay if you apply for refugee status, but so many Somalis have fled here, and Kenyans think you're all terrorists. The police are told to do something about "the Somali problem", so they arrest random Somalis without visas and throw them back across the border. I wouldn't like to see that happen to you.'

You sigh heavily. How can people here think all Somalis are terrorists, when most Somalis are *fleeing* terrorists?

Sampson has been so wonderful and generous. You had hoped that you could stay in the safety of his shop for longer. But the threat of al-Shabaab has followed you, even here. You wonder if you'll ever truly feel safe and free again.

A flurry of customers come into the shop, and Sampson gets busy serving them while you and Jamilah get busy putting price tags on items and unpacking vegetables. By the afternoon, Sampson's naturally affable and laid-back disposition has returned, and he no longer seems worried about the morning's blunder.

'Let's wait and see, my darlings,' says Sampson, opening a packet of Manji Ginger Snaps. 'There's no need to call the police – I'm sure things will work out fine. *Mwanamaji akimbia wimbi?* Will the sailor flee from the waves? You're still safe here. Have a biscuit.'

Jamilah takes three and grins at Sampson.

She thinks anywhere there are biscuits is a good place to stay, you think ruefully.

You're not so sure, though.

✦ To insist that Sampson calls the police, turn to page 104.

✦ To wait and see what happens without calling the police, as Sampson suggests, turn to page 107.

Why would this stranger believe your story about the pen? You decide to run. You grab Jamilah's arm and jump up from the bench. The man steps into your path, but you push past him and begin to run through the park towards the street.

'Hey,' he shouts, 'I'm not going to hurt you! Kids!'

People are turning to look as you race by. A middle-aged man in a suit makes a grab for you. You dodge him. A woman walking along the path with a little girl jumps out of your way, yanking the girl, who stumbles and begins to cry. You are attracting a commotion and you haven't even been in the city for one whole morning.

You make it to the far side of the park and back onto the street and slow to a walk, trying to blend in.

But the lady with the little girl has followed you. She shouts something in Swahili: – '*Mwizi! Mtoto ya nyoka ni nyoka,*' she spits. People look at you in disgust.

To your horror, you see a couple of policemen approach. The woman raises her arm, points straight at you and Jamilah, and shouts: '*Mwizi!*'

You sprint again, yanking Jamilah with you, but the footpath is too crowded, and the police catch you.

'Somali?' they ask, in English, pointing at you. You nod. 'Identity card?'

You don't have one. Of course not.

They search your pockets and find the pen. You try to explain, but they won't believe it's not stolen. They keep it and shove you into a van. Their job is to get Somali refugees without papers out of Nairobi.

You think of the Kenyan news headlines Aunty Rahama read to you over the last few months:

Kenya rocked by bombs in Nairobi terror attacks.

Somalis in Kenya find themselves under suspicion.

Kenya deports Somalis, arrests hundreds in crackdown after attacks.

These aren't headlines anymore – they're pieces of your story. As the van rumbles through the streets, you bang on the wall that separates you from the driver and shout: 'You have to let us stay, please! We are running *away* from the terrorists. We're even more afraid of them than you Kenyans are!'

As you and Jamilah are herded into Pangani Police Station, fingerprinted, and locked in a cell, none of the officials speak to you. Not with their voices. But their body language shouts: *You're scum. You're weeds. Get out and never come back.*

The only other person in your cell is a thin man

with vacant eyes and dirty clothes. He's licking his finger and rubbing at his skin, muttering: 'It never comes out, it never comes out.'

'What's wrong with him?' whispers Jamilah. 'He's scary.'

He hears her, and his eyes snap upwards and lock onto you. 'They tattooed me,' he says in Somali. 'See, here on my skin, these words.'

You look at the man's skin, but there's nothing there, only a bruise where he's been rubbing.

The hairs stand up on the back of your neck. You don't want to talk to him, but your curiosity wins out. 'What do the words say?' you ask him.

'Terrorist,' he spits. 'Vermin, parasite, illegal. Somali scum.' You shudder. 'They'll put them on you too,' he mutters. 'They will.'

You know that, although the man is deluded, those words are yours and Jamilah's now too. You belong nowhere: not here in Kenya, and not home in Somalia, where al-Shabaab wants you dead. There is no space between the borders where a pair of unwanted kids might rest.

THE END

✦ To return to your last choice and try again, go to page 89.

'No, Sampson, you need to call the police,' you insist. 'Trust me – Arsenal are and deadly. You really might be in danger. And besides, if the police take us seriously, they might be able to make use of this information and do something about shutting down Bright Dream and al-Shabaab.'

Sampson tries to persuade you and Jamilah to hide from the police. He wants to concoct a story about how a customer left the pen in his shop, but there would be too many holes in his story.

'How will you explain how you worked out what the internet banking password was?' you ask him.

Besides, you want to talk to the police yourself. You've gone through a lot of danger to bring this information out of Somalia, and you want to make sure that they take it seriously. You just hope they won't throw you and Jamilah out of the country.

The two police officers who come to the shop look stern and sceptical in their blue uniforms. There's a small, wiry man and a woman with hair that looks as tough and tightly curled as a pot-scourer. Luckily they speak English.

'We'll have to take this pen into the office to investigate its contents,' Pot-Scourer says once you've finished telling them your story. 'Are you sure you don't know how to get into the password-protected file?'

'Yes, I'm sure,' you say, 'but I'm afraid you can't have the pen.'

Sampson persuades them to copy its contents onto a second memory stick he has spare. The police agree, and they also make assurances that they will give Sampson's shop extra surveillance in case al-Shabaab tracks him down from the banking log-in.

'For the children's safety, it would be best if we send them to Dadaab,' says the wiry man to Sampson. 'Just in case al-Shabaab have tracked them this far. They can apply for refugee status with the UNHCR there.'

You've heard of Dadaab. It's a Kenyan refugee camp close to the Somali–Kenya border. It's in the middle of the desert – the last resort for thousands of people for whom the only other choice was death. If you can't stay in Nairobi, then Dadaab would be better than being sent home. You're just not sure *how* much better.

Sampson begs the police to treat you well, as they

begin to lead you and Jamilah away. He follows you out the door, filling both your pockets with biscuits and drinks for the trip to Dadaab.

He kisses your forehead, then Jamilah's. She is crying. You are trying not to.

'Good luck, children,' he says as you're dragged out the door. '*Anipa mungu kwa kadiri yangu: God gives you a load to carry to the extent of your strength.* I know you will be strong enough for whatever may come next.'

'I love you, Uncle Sammy!' Jamilah hiccups. You see the police officers exchange a soft look with each other.

'All right,' Wiry Guy says, clearing his throat. 'There's a ride to Dadaab that leaves every few hours from the market. You can stay the night at the police station, and we'll put you on that first thing tomorrow. Now let's get you out of here.'

<hr />

✦ To read a fact file on refugees and asylum seekers, turn to page 313, then go to page 112 to continue with the story.
✦ To continue with the story now, go to page 112.

It's just so tempting to believe that Sampson is right: that al-Shabaab won't find you here; that they won't be able to trace the glimpse you got of their bank account. Sampson's big belly puts you in mind of a bear – a relaxed, protective uncle bear. You want to believe that no harm could come to you in this safe country, Kenya, in this brightly lit shop filled with good things to eat, under the friendly gaze of Sampson. You agree not to call the police.

You go on with your day. Jamilah has a little nap behind the counter. You fill in an order form for next week's supplies, under Sampson's guidance. A group of women come into the shop looking for henna to dye their palms for a wedding ceremony, and Sampson is busily helping them when two men come in too, their faces wrapped in chequered scarves, reflective sunglasses covering their eyes. One of them raises a gun.

The customers squeal and run out. You see Jamilah wake with a start and hide in a cupboard under the counter, and you duck and squeeze into a tiny gap between the wall and the refrigerator.

Sampson rushes to confront the men.

'Tell us why you logged in to Bright Dream's bank account,' snarls one of the men in Somali.

'What's Bright Dream?' asks Sampson. 'I never log in to any bank account but my own!'

'This computer was reported to have been used to access *our* bank account,' growls the other man, the one with the gun, waving it in the direction of Sampson's computer. 'We never authorised that.'

'Of course not,' replies Sampson, 'but it could have been any of my customers. As well as being a shop, I'm something of an internet cafe. My customers often log on here to use email, YouTube, Facebook—'

'We get the picture,' snaps the first man. 'You should pay more attention to who is using your computer. Who was on it at six o'clock this morning?'

'I have no idea,' says Sampson firmly. 'Now please leave my shop.'

The man with the gun raises it, and you stuff your fist into your mouth to stop yourself from screaming. But instead of shooting Sampson, he shoots his computer. Shards of glass explode everywhere, and the monitor catches fire with a crackling sound.

The man shoots the computer again. Pieces of metal fly through the air, and the bullet embeds itself in the wall behind it with a dull *crack*.

The men leave the shop without another word. They shoot the glass doors as they go, sending a tinkling cascade of glass to the floor.

Sampson puts out the fire with a blanket. 'Are you okay, children?' he calls.

'Yes!' you shout back.

You squeeze out of the gap you were hiding in and run for Jamilah's cupboard. You help her out and she huddles in a corner behind the counter, hugging her knees and rocking back and forth.

'Jamilah?' you ask, cupping her chin in your hand. She won't look at you. 'It's okay. They've gone.'

Still she won't talk. She just carries on rocking and staring blankly ahead. Tears are running down her face.

How much can we take? you wonder. *How many times can our safety be broken before we never feel safe again?*

You made a promise to Rahama to protect your little sister, but *how*? Nowhere seems safe now.

You don't know what else to do, so you begin sweeping up the glass from the doors to help Sampson.

A small crowd has gathered outside, gossiping and pointing. 'I've called the police!' someone shouts.

You turn to Sampson. 'I'm so sorry,' you say. 'I had no idea they could track us down here.'

'I know,' he replies and sighs. His voice is kind but weary. 'It sounds like the police are on their way. Don't worry about my shop – I'll find a way to pay for it. But the police can't find you here. They could throw you out of the country. I've been thinking,' he goes on, 'that perhaps the best place for you is Dadaab.'

'The refugee camp near the border?' you ask in a small voice.

'They have schools there,' Sampson says, 'and aid organisations that can look after unaccompanied children. You can get protection and an education.'

You hear a police siren approaching. It looks like you don't have much choice. Sampson quickly opens the till and gives you a wad of notes.

'Trucks leave the central marketplace for Dadaab a few times every day,' he tells you in a rushed voice. 'Take the 407 bus from out the front, it goes straight there. Use this money for the truck fare. Safe travels, my dears. I'm so sorry I can't do more.'

You go to grab Jamilah from her hiding place, but she suddenly rushes past you and squeezes Sampson's legs so tightly that he has to put a hand on a shelf to keep his balance.

'I love you, Uncle Sammy,' she sobs.

Sampson's eyes are full of tears too. He starts stuffing your and Jamilah's pockets full of drinks and snacks for the trip. You check that Rahama's pen is also still in your pocket – it is.

You manage to dash out the door before the police arrive, but by the time you reach the marketplace, the last bus for Dadaab has already left. You spend the night in the deserted marketplace, waiting for the dawn.

✳ To read a fact file about refugees and asylum seekers, go to page 313, then go to page 112 to continue with the story.

✳ To continue with the story now, go to page 112.

The next morning, you get a ride to Dadaab in the open bed of a truck, with about sixty other Somalis, but no other kids. You all jam in together. A couple of elderly people sit down, but everyone else has to stand.

At first, you concentrate on getting Jamilah to look around at the city, then the countryside, trying to distract her from her tears. You encourage her to eat some of Sampson's snacks. Eventually, though, all your energy ebbs away and you just concentrate on keeping you both upright in the crowd, despite your aching legs and the sand stinging your face.

You're in the middle of the desert now. The truck doesn't stop for anything – the driver doesn't care if his passengers need to pee or stretch their legs. He might not even notice or care if one of you falls off, condemning you to a slow, dry death in the desert. The crowd tightens like one single creature sucking itself in whenever the truck hits a pothole and lurches.

It is both a relief and a disappointment to see the outlines of Dadaab refugee camp in the distance. By this time the sun is low in the sky, and the smoke from cooking fires and the dust around the camp envelop it in an amber cloud.

You're reminded of the little pretend towns you and Jamilah used to make in the dirt: clods of earth for the homes; thorns stuck in the ground for fences; and little twigs for people, wearing clothes of dried leaves.

But then you get closer and see the mind-boggling size of the place. Greyish-white dome tents are dotted over the red sand as far as the eye can see. The truck rumbles deeper into the camp. It goes on forever.

There are mothers with clinging babies stoking fires, and boys playing soccer with a paper-and-string ball like you and your schoolfriends used to make in Mogadishu. Ragged men carry heavy sacks. Better-dressed men go in and out of occasional more solid buildings, brightly painted with logos: 'CARE', 'UNHCR'. Once you even see a white person climbing into a four-wheel drive.

Layer after layer of people have hunkered down here, embedding themselves in the landscape, wrapping shelters and hammering fences and making more babies and deeper roads, until there is this: a thick human settlement of tents and tin, hundreds of thousands of people clinging to life in a land of nothing but sand. Now you are one of them.

WEEKS PASS. WHEN you arrived, you and Jamilah were passed from one agency to another, in a string of registrations and queues and fingerprinting and health checks. Now you have been given a shelter for the two of you – one of the grey-white dome tents, with a sandy floor. There is nothing in the tent besides a little pot for water, and the sticks you collect for a fire. You sleep on the bare ground.

You are each given about a handful of beans and a handful of rice every day, gained after standing in line for hours with little cardboard tags around your necks, which get a hole punched in them in return for the food. You have long since eaten Sampson's snacks and spent the last of your money on extra food and a blanket, and you are always hungry.

Rahama's pen gleams on, the ruby so red it looks edible. You've started school, in a crowded metal shed where fifty boys sit together on a concrete floor, but you couldn't take the golden pen out to write with there – it would be stolen in an instant. You keep it wrapped in paper and buried under the sand in a corner of the tent, showing it to no one.

What is the point of having something so beautiful in a place like this? you think bitterly. *It just makes everything else look uglier.*

YOU'VE BEEN IN Dadaab for months, learning how to survive and get by. Sometimes you hear rumours that al-Shabaab agents are mixed in among the camp's population – plotting, spying, and recruiting – so you don't tell anyone the story of why you're here. When you tell the UNHCR your story, you simply say that you were fleeing the famine.

You and Jamilah keep your heads down and blend in, and you feel safer here than anywhere else you've been so far. However, you still often lie awake at night, filled with a restless frustration. *I can't stay in Dadaab forever*, you think. *I have to get in touch with Aadan; I have to investigate Bright Dream.*

But you know now, from talking to people around the camp, that most people simply run out of options and never leave Dadaab. There are people of your parents' generation who were born here, Somalis who've never set foot in Somalia. The only way to get from here to a truly safe place is to wait for the UNHCR to resettle you in an overseas country, but getting a resettlement place is like winning the lottery.

If only you could call Sampson, or use a computer to contact Aadan. But the only computers and phones here in Dadaab are impossibly expensive to use.

Some people starve themselves and sell their rations in the marketplace as a way of making money. Maybe you will have to try doing that. *I have the pen,* you always think, *but I can't sell that.*

One day an idea occurs to you, so simple you can't believe you haven't thought of it before now: *I could sell* half *the pen – the writing half – and keep the part with the ruby and the memory stick!*

You send Jamilah off to school the next morning but skip class yourself. You don't want to tell her about your plan until it works and you have some really good news for her.

Dadaab's central market, nicknamed 'Bosnia', is a sprawling labyrinth of dirt footpaths and trestle tables piled high with goods, from tomatoes to baby clothes to glistening lumps of camel meat. It buzzes with the voices of stallholders hawking their wares, the squawking of chickens destined for the chop, the clunking of vans being unloaded, and the occasional trill of a bicycle bell as a rider weaves through the crowd.

Most of the market has a makeshift ceiling of plastic bags and rags to keep out the desert sun, and you very quickly become disoriented in the maze of crowded tunnels. You have no idea who would be a trustworthy person to approach about selling your half-pen.

A mountain of potatoes atop a wildly weaving wheelbarrow charges towards you. The load is so huge that you can't even see the person pushing it.

You jump out of the way just in time, and a wiry, sweating man in a red T-shirt shouts, 'Make way, make way!' as he throws his full bodyweight into the load.

You watch, amazed by the spectacle. Just at that moment, the wheelbarrow-pusher swerves violently and only just manages to right his load in time. He shouts angrily at a man with a huge sack who got in his way – then, to your horror, he smacks the man across the face, making him drop his sack, before charging on.

You run to the man who was hit. 'Are you all right?' you ask in Somali.

But then you realise he isn't Somali – his skin is pitch-black and he has tribal scars on his forehead. *Maybe he's Sudanese*, you think, and try asking again in Arabic.

He smiles. 'I'm all right, thanks kid,' he replies,

in accented Arabic. 'That'll teach me for getting in the way of a stampeding herd of potatoes.'

You laugh and begin to help him pick up the contents of his sack: used cans, bottles and other bits of rubbish. Then you notice that he reaches for the rubbish with only one hand: the other arm ends in a gum-pink stump at the wrist. You gasp in horror, then feel embarrassed.

'Don't be frightened, kid,' he says kindly. 'I'm Jok.'

He offers you his left hand, and you shake it awkwardly. Jok picks up the now-full sack at its neck, and swings it over his shoulder.

'You ever see any cans or bottles lying around here, you bring them right to me, okay?' he grins.

'Why?'

'Well, because I'm Scavenger Jok, that's why. I collect stuff. Everything in my sack gets used again or sold. That's how I get by. I'll give you a coin if you bring me something good.'

A coin! you think. *Maybe I won't have to sell half the pen after all.*

You spend the rest of the day running all over the camp hunting down anything that could be reused or recycled: tin, string, screws, half a plastic thong, the tough blue tape from around the food supply boxes.

'You have a good eye for scavenging,' Jok tells you at the end of the day when you find him again. He hands you a Kenyan five-shilling coin: not nearly enough to make a phone call, but a good start. 'Still, I think you should have been in school today, no?'

You shrug. 'I have more important things to do.'

'Ha!' Jok shouts. 'Nothing is more important than getting an education, kid – d'you hear me?'

He squeezes your hand strongly with his good one.

'Come back and find me at Bosnia over the weekend, if you want to make more money. But don't you show up during school time, or I'll put *you* in my sack and carry you there myself!'

Smiling, you promise.

AFTER SCHOOL AND on weekends over the next couple of months, you and Jamilah become Scavenger Jok's sidekicks. Your aim is to make three hundred Kenyan shillings for phone calls and computer access, and you're steadily getting there.

Jamilah is even faster and sharper-eyed than you are at finding rubbish for Jok, and in your wanderings, you see a lot of the camp. Doing this work for Jok makes you feel like nothing is wasted:

everything has a purpose. Jok sometimes tells you stories of life in his home county, or Sudanese folktales, but you're too shy to ask how he lost his hand.

Dadaab will always be dusty, and dry, and crowded, but now you begin to see how hard people here try to get ahead – how resourceful they are. You begin to admire the mothers lugging babies on their hips, the porters from Bosnia market bent double under sacks of charcoal, the imam whose mosque is a tin shed but who carries on blessing the newly born and the dying every day.

'I've been thinking,' you say to Jok one day. 'Everyone here lives in tents and huts with no windows. It isn't safe to cut a hole in the wall or canvas to let in light, and there isn't any glass to make a window that you can open and close. So it's always dark and dingy inside.'

'That's true,' agrees Jok.

'What if we use some of these bottles to make a light?' you say, holding up a plastic bottle half full of water. You've been throwing and catching it as you walk, noticing how the light sparkles from it. 'If you had one of these water bottles in your ceiling, it would catch the light and beam it all over your hut.'

'Wow – good idea!' Jok exclaims. 'Let's try it on my hut first.'

You, Jok and Jamilah rush back to Jok's hut to try it out. His wife, a curvy, brightly dressed woman called Adut who is always kind to you, is very sceptical about cutting a hole in their roof, but Jok convinces her.

Together, you and Jok carefully use a rusty pair of tin-snips to cut a hole the right size in Jok's roof. Jok tips more water into the bottle until it's full, and Adut thinks to add some soap powder to keep the water from stagnating. Jok then tightens the lid, and inserts the upright bottle into the hole.

Jamilah squeals happily. 'It works, it works!'

'This is amazing!' exclaims Jok. Light is filtering through the bottle and now illuminates the inside of his hut. 'It's so simple!'

You climb onto his roof, seal around the edges of the hole with some melted plastic, and the job is done.

'Everyone should have one of these!' says Adut. 'I know my friends will all want one.'

And she's right. Some people copy the idea and make their own bottle lights for free, but many more pay you and Jok to provide the bottle and install it for them.

By the end of that week, you have enough money to use a phone and a computer.

I've done it, you think triumphantly. *And I still have the whole pen. I'll call Sampson tomorrow after school.*

The thought that you might be talking to Sampson, and then Aadan in Australia, by the end of tomorrow makes your stomach dance.

That night, you dig in the dirt in the corner of your tent and take out the pen. There's just enough moonlight coming through the tent's doorway to write with, and there's a piece of paper in your pocket – a label from one of the bottles you picked up earlier.

You write with the pen for the first time. A poem that has been forming in your mind these last few days now flows like quicksilver onto the back of the label.

I HAVE A DREAM
A dream that will never fail.
Wasn't every successful person
Once a dreamer like me?
Wasn't every great tree that the wind blows
Once a tiny seed?
My dreams are just like a seed
Fallen on a rocky path.
My journey is long

But I do not waver.
Every day of my life is a page of my history.
Every day the seed spreads its roots.
Every step that I take is a move
Towards my glorious destiny.
As the seed becomes a tree
It's not where I am
But how I'm growing that matters.
Now listen carefully to these words of wisdom:
Stop watching your dreams fall.
Fight.
Fight.
Fight for your dreams.
Fall down seven times and get up eight times.
Wasn't every successful person once a dreamer
    like me?
Wasn't every great tree that the wind blows
Once a tiny seed?

✳ To read an interview with Hani Abdile, the young Somali woman who really wrote this poem, go to page 324.

✳ To read a fact file on bottle-lights and other great inventions, and find out who really invented the plastic bottle-light, go to page 315.

✳ To continue with the story, go to page 124.

The next morning, you leave for school in high spirits, knowing that by the afternoon, you'll at least be talking to Sampson, if not Aadan in Australia too.

Because Jamilah is young, she finishes school before you do, so you've told her you'll meet her back at the tent that afternoon, then you'll go together to make the call.

You're tempted to skip school and call right now, but you promised Jok you wouldn't skip class for any reason. You and Jamilah feel like part of his family now, so you take that promise seriously. Jok and Adut had their own children, six of them, but they were all out collecting water when Sudanese terrorists – the Janjaweed – rode into their village and torched it. Adut and Jok had no choice but to run, and they never saw their children again. They don't know if they are dead or alive.

Unfortunately, not everyone thinks as highly of Jok as you do: his one hand, his distinctive looks, his job picking up rubbish, and his Sudanese background in a mainly Somali camp have all marked him as an outsider.

There's a group of four boys in your class, the rudest and cockiest ones, who think they're better than everyone else, because they were born here in Dadaab. They have noticed your friendship with Jok, and they tease you for it, calling him One-hand Jok and you Jok's Other Hand, or just Stink Boy. They hold their noses when you enter the room, and pick on you any chance they get.

Today, you're dismayed to see when you arrive that the only spot left to sit on the concrete floor is right next to them. The tallest boy, Yasir, tries to trip you as you walk past him, and the others snigger.

As the lesson begins, Dayib, who always wears a yellow baseball hat that says 'Michigan General Motors' on it, drops a note in your lap. It has a poem scrawled on it.

> *One-hand Jok, One-hand Jok,*
> *smells like the rubbish that's in his sack.*
> *One-hand Jok, One-hand Jok,*
> *ugliest of ugly and blackest of the black.*
> *Jok's Other Hand also smells like poo.*
> *We guess his mummy must have crapped him*
> *out, too.*

You *hate* how these boys are racist towards Jok like that. But if they want you to get upset at a stupid prejudiced poem about *poo*, of all things, they have another think coming.

'At least call it by its real name,' you whisper, and you cross out 'poo' and scribble a really foul Somali swearword for diarrhoea over the top. After all you've been through, it's not like you're going to fall apart and cry over a rude poem.

But it gets worse. The teacher sees you pass the note and gives both you and General Motors a strong smack across the palm with a bamboo cane, in front of the whole class. The humiliation hurts more than the cane.

The four boys corner you after class that day, just as you're in a desperate rush to get away and make the phone call.

'Did you leave Somalia because of the famine, Stink Boy? No wonder you've got legs like sticks and your brain rattles around in your head!'

'Is that why you walk around picking up rubbish? You think it will be good to eat? Num num num!'

'Here, eat this, Stink Boy!' A shower of pebbles and dirt patters over you.

'Eat *this*!' A larger stone strikes your shin.

Their nasty taunts make you ball up your fists, and a fire is growing in your belly – you want to crush them like bugs! But you really can't afford to be held up today.

Then you remember you have a pocketful of the coins you've been saving for the phone calls. Instead of fighting them, you could throw one on the ground – they would all dive for it, and you could get away. But that would leave you short for the calls...

✳ To fight the gang, go to page 128.

✳ To try to distract the boys with money, go to page 144.

The sparks in your belly are leaping higher and higher, now fuelled by a bonfire of rage. You won't risk your hard-earned money. You're ready for a fight. But you have something to say first.

'You think you're better than me somehow because you were born here?' you shout. 'Think that makes you special? Big deal! It doesn't!'

'Shut up, Stink Boy,' sneers Yasir. 'You have nothing. No family, no girlfriend, no future.'

You don't let it show, but the taunt about your family cuts you inside. The loss of Aunty Rahama is still a raw, aching hole that never goes away. Then you think of Jamilah, and a fierce, protective love burns even brighter than the fire inside you.

'I have more than you could ever dream of! I have my sister, and we're going to Australia! You know nothing about me! You think I'm some useless kid, but I escaped from al-Shabaab! They killed my Aunty Rahama because she was an awesome journalist who knew secrets that could destroy them! What does *your* mum do?'

'Don't you talk about my mum, you little piece of crap,' snarls General Motors, advancing towards you. His three friends also raise their fists.

You fly at them, and you're soon tangled in a net of fists and yells. In no time you're down on the ground, sand in your eyes.

You feel some of your coins tumble out of your pocket onto the ground and hope desperately that they don't notice them, but they do. All five of you are now scrabbling in the dirt, trying to grab as many coins as you can.

Then Yasir shouts, 'Teacher!' and they all leap up and scatter, leaving you alone in the dust.

You sit up and take juddering breaths until you can breathe easily again. You managed to grab most of the coins, but you're about a hundred shillings down now – a third of all your and Jamilah's hard work. You put your hand to your face and feel a puffy warm lump around one eye.

Jamilah looks scared when you get home and she takes in the sight of you. You fill her in on what happened in a dull voice. Then you lie down and close your eyes, your mess of disappointment and anger fading into a bone-heavy tiredness, and you don't wake again until after dark.

When you wake, the first thing you see is Jamilah's

small shoulders under her blanket next to you. She hears you stir and sits up.

'Are you okay?' she asks in a little voice.

'I feel fine,' you lie. 'What about you? It's late, did you eat dinner?'

'I had it at Aunty's,' she replies. Jamilah has found a friend – a Somali woman who lives several tents down from yours, who Jamilah calls Aunty. Aunty's children died in the famine, and she seems very attached to Jamilah. She sings her songs and gives her little treats, like a pencil for school, a piece of dried fruit, or a shiny bangle. Jamilah adores her.

'Okay then,' you say. You lie back down and think about the fact that your shirt is now crusty with dirt. It's your only one. You will have to miss a morning of school tomorrow to try to wash it properly with the little water you have in your tent.

You manage to make it to school by the next afternoon, in a clean-ish shirt. You take a seat on the other side of the room from the boys, and you ignore each other. After school, you rush out to avoid them, going straight to Jok's hut and making a start on working through the long list of people waiting for one of your bottle-lamps.

When you get back to your tent around dinnertime,

Jamilah isn't there. She must be at Aunty's. You walk down to get her.

Sure enough, there's Aunty, braiding Jamilah's hair and singing a soothing song. Jamilah looks worried. Her little brow is furrowed, and she's twisting her fingers around her skirt. There are thin lines of dried-up tears on her cheeks.

'What's wrong?' you ask.

She doesn't reply. Aunty does. 'Tsk, you should have been home this afternoon. Poor little Jamilah needed you.'

'Why? What happened?' you ask, your heart rising into your throat.

Please be okay, you think. *Please be okay*. The camp is not a safe place, especially for young women and girls.

'Two men came to our tent,' whispers Jamilah.

'It's all right, they didn't attack her,' says Aunty. 'They frightened her, though.'

'They said they knew I was Rahama Daahir's niece,' she says. 'They asked where you were.'

Al-Shabaab. The secret you let slip during your fight with the boys has spread fast. You feel sick to the stomach. Then a thought strikes you.

'The pen! Where is it, Jamilah?'

'It's all right,' says Aunty again, still braiding

Jamilah's hair. 'After the men left, she brought it straight to me. It's lovely – is it real gold?'

'Oh, no,' you lie. 'Definitely not.' You don't want Aunty to think it's worth anything.

'Still, it's very nice – amazing you've kept it all this while. Jamilah asked me to keep it safe. Something to do with … Arsenal?'

The reference to al-Shabaab makes your stomach drop. 'Um,' you say. You don't know Aunty very well, and you don't know what to do. If you could trust her with the truth, it would be good to hide the pen with her – al-Shabaab won't think to look for it here. But what's to say she won't just steal the pen and sell it, or even worse, betray you to al-Shabaab?

You notice that Jamilah is hugging one of Aunty's skinny, dry legs as Aunty continues to braid her hair.

Aunty looks up at you.

'Well?' she asks.

✦ If you admit the truth and ask Aunty to help you keep the pen safe from al-Shabaab, go to page 133.

✦ If you take the pen back and lie about its origins, go to page 138.

*J*amilah *loves Aunty so much,* you reason to yourself. *And Aunty thinks of her like her own child. She wouldn't betray us.*

So you tell her everything.

Aunty's eyes grow wide as she listens. She nods, and says supportive things like, 'Wow! You poor children,' and, 'So what happened next?'

You find that it's an immense relief to be able to tell another adult your story – someone who really wants to listen; who comes from your country and truly understands what it's like there. She's the first person you've told since you came to Dadaab; you haven't even told Jok.

'I hate Arsenal, I really do,' Aunty says when you're finished. 'Anything I can do to weaken them would be an honour.'

You feel strange to leave the pen in her care, but you can have it back anytime you want it, and this way if the al-Shabaab guys come looking for you again, they won't find anything.

Now you just have to hide yourselves. But where?

After all, Dadaab is a place for people who have run out of other places to escape to.

'You can stay here with me tonight,' offers Aunty.

'Thank you so much,' you say. 'But we should move to a different part of the camp – further away from here.'

'We could go to Scavenger Jok's,' says Jamilah.

You don't want to bring trouble to Jok and Adut's home, but you can't think of a better idea.

Jok and Adut are stricken with worry when they hear your story. Jok has tears in his eyes, and Jamilah starts crying too. It's as if you're both in danger of losing your families all over again.

'Of course you can stay as long as you want,' says Jok.

'But the safest place in the camp,' suggests Adut, 'is probably with the UNHCR. They have a little group of houses locked behind big fences, with a security guard. You're allowed to stay there if you can prove your life is in danger in the camp.'

In the morning, Jok gives you the money for a mini-bus fare to the UNHCR buildings. Dadaab is so vast that it would take you and Jamilah hours to walk there.

'First though,' you tell Jamilah, 'we'll go to Aunty's and get the pen, so we can prove to the UNHCR that they need to let us stay in the locked section.'

But as soon as you approach Aunty's tent, you realise something is wrong. There's no cloth hanging to dry outside on the line, no smoke wisping from the cooking fire, no hum of her voice – the place is silent as a grave.

'Wait there,' you tell Jamilah, and she stands out on the road while you duck inside Aunty's tent.

You gasp. Two men are sitting inside, and they stand as you come in. 'Where's Aunty?' you demand. 'Did you kill her?'

They just laugh. 'Your "aunty" realised she could afford much more than a tent in Dadaab if she sold us a little treasure we've been looking for,' says one of the men in a soft, oily voice.

He reaches into his pocket and pulls out your pen. It lies in his palm, glinting red and gold like the setting sun.

You look to the doorway. Your little sister is standing there, frozen with confusion. She hasn't realised yet what this means – she's still too little and trusting to realise that Aunty has sold you out to al-Shabaab, and that now they have what they were after from you, you are about to die.

'Run!' you shout. 'Go, Jamilah!' She disappears

from the doorway and the second man whips a gun from his pocket, but she is gone.

'We'll catch her,' says the man with the gun. Then you make a leap for the door, but his bullet hits your chest before you can even take two steps.

The men stand up, the oily-voiced one slipping your pen back into his pocket. Their two black shadows loom over you. They are watching to make sure you are dead.

But I'm not dead, you think.

You can hear a drumbeat calling you to dance. It's the sound of your own heart, and it booms through your body like an ancient song. The shadows of the men are dancing like black ribbons. Your feet move as though you were a stone skipping over water.

You can hear a song: a cry of the desert that wails and swoops like an eagle. A woman's voice sings, full of sorrow.

Oh, my son, you have come through the desert.

How you must long to rest your head.

Oh, my son, I know you are tired.

I will bring you pure water and my own fresh bread.

Oh, my son, I see your tears falling.

I know how you've struggled and what you've been through.

Come, my son, and let me dry them…

…in the garden where love can be born anew.

The drumbeat slows, and you know the dance is at an end. You recognise the singer's voice now – it's that of your mother. You haven't heard it since you were a child.

You close your eyes, ready for the last of the pain to fall away. The tall black shadows depart. The drumming of your heart stops.

THE END

✦ To return to your last choice and try again, go to the page 132.

You've come this far looking after the pen on your own. You decide you'd rather keep it yourself for now.

'It's just a trinket that belonged to our aunt,' you say. 'But I know it looks valuable, so sometimes I worry that it might be stolen. Our aunt was a student, and she gave it to me as a reminder to always work hard on my education. It's not worth anything, but it does mean a lot to me. I write poems with it sometimes. Please may I have it back?'

'Oh, so it has nothing to do with Arsenal?' asks Aunty with a raised eyebrow. 'Because Jamilah told me—'

'Jamilah's scared of Arsenal, so when our aunt gave it to us, she told us it would keep us safe from the bad guys. Like a lucky charm,' you lie. 'You know, Jamilah still believes in it...'

You smile confidentially, playing the part of the older, wiser brother, and ruffle your sister's newly braided hair. It feels bumpy, like a fuzzy corncob. Jamilah pulls her hijab up over it and scowls at you.

'Those men were probably just friends of Aunty Rahama's from home, visiting to ask after her,' you say to Jamilah. 'That's why they knew her name. Don't worry, I'm here now. Let's go home, and I'll make dinner.'

Aunty hands the pen to you without another word.

Jamilah huffs and kicks the dust as you walk home.

'Why didn't you tell Aunty the truth?' she mutters furiously. 'You made me look like a dumb little kid who believes in magic pens!'

'I'm sorry,' you say, because you know you made her look foolish. 'But it's better if no one knows about our secret, not even Aunty. Arsenal could be anywhere, listening in.'

You're afraid to return to your tent, but you've decided not to trust Aunty, and it's a long walk across the camp at night-time to Jok's. You decide that would be even more dangerous than staying put. You try to pretend things are all right for Jamilah's sake as you settle down for the night in your tent, but you can't sleep.

You sneak out once she's asleep, back to Aunty's tent. You can't shake the feeling that she didn't swallow your lie.

A little orange glow from a kerosene lamp filters through the cracks of her tent and onto the sand. You hear low voices talking.

'Just eight tents down that way,' you hear Aunty's voice murmur. 'A pen made of gold with a ruby in the end. The little girl said it was her Aunty Rahama's and it held a secret...'

Your hear men's voices conferring so softly you can't make out what they're saying.

'My money?' asks Aunty. 'You promised it to me, and I need it.'

You sprint back to your tent and drag Jamilah upright.

'Whassup?' she mumbles.

'Quiet! Follow me!' you hiss. 'Al-Shabaab are after us.'

You have the pen and your money in your pocket, and you're both wearing your only set of clothes. You'll have to leave your schoolbooks and the pot you cook on behind.

Jamilah stumbles out of your tent, her blanket around her shoulders. You see black figures coming down the path from the direction of Aunty's tent, and you shove Jamilah through the gap between the two tents behind yours.

Bending double, your arm on Jamilah's back,

pressing her down too, you start to run, weaving between tents until you reach a wider road.

'Run with me to Jok's place,' you whisper to Jamilah. 'Al-Shabaab are after us.'

You make it to Jok's hut in record time. His hut has a door, which he unlocks to let you in.

At first, you and Jamilah are shaking so much that you can't get the words out to explain to him why you're there. But after a cup of tea, Jamilah eventually falls asleep curled at the end of his bed like a cat, while you, Jok and Adut stay awake talking. You're certain you can trust them, and you show them the pen and tell them what's on it.

'I never told you how I lost this hand,' says Jok, nodding to his stump. 'You already know that the Janjaweed torched our village. After we escaped, and Adut and I were on the run, I was caught stealing grain from their soldiers' supplies for us to survive. This was my punishment. They could have killed me, but they left me alive as an example to others.'

You shudder, and lay a hand on Jok's arm. 'I'm sorry,' you say.

It's not fair, you think. *Why do innocent people have to suffer so much, while the bad guys get away with it?*

You know that some preachers promise fair rewards and punishments will be dished out in the afterlife, but that's little comfort right now.

THE NEXT MORNING, you wake to a pale dawn light radiating from the bottle-lamp in Jok's ceiling. You wake Jamilah, wash, and both perform morning prayers. Prayer is your one daily constant: a link to home and Allah. Adut kneels beside you and murmurs her own prayers in her native Dinka language.

'Don't go out today,' says Jok. 'Stay hidden here. The UNHCR has a locked compound on the other side of Dadaab where they can accommodate people whose lives are being threatened. I'm going to go there, and see if they can help us.'

Around noon, you hear a distant *boom* and *crunch*. The last time you heard a bomb go off was when Aunty Rahama was killed – it's not a sound you forget easily. Your stomach curdles. Jamilah clutches Adut's hand.

People scream and cars honk. You pray Jok was nowhere near it. To your relief, he runs in the door soon after.

'Al-Shabaab planted a bomb in the road,' he pants.

'A UNHCR car drove over it, and some foreign-aid workers were killed. People are saying they're trying to scare off all the aid workers – that maybe they'll kidnap and execute some of them too, until they all leave and the camp can't function. Then they'll round up Somali boys to use as soldiers back in your country, and kill anyone who objects. We have to get you out of here. Forget the UNHCR – I have a plan.'

You and Jok pool your savings and, leaving Jamilah and Adut at home, run to the edge of Bosnia, where you know there's a small shop at which you can pay to use the internet and phone.

By the blue light of the screen of a beat-up laptop, you find the phone number of Sampson's shop in Eastleigh. The grizzled, stinky proprietor of the shop hands over his phone, and you call Sampson's number.

Please pick up, you think. *Please, please, please.*

◇═◈══◇═══◇══◈═◇

✦ To continue with the story, go to page 151.

You slip a hand inside your pocket and your fingers find a couple of coins. As you hoped, as soon as you throw them onto the ground the four guys dive for them, giving you enough time to jump aside and sprint away.

You're so angry that they've cost you a little of your money, but hopefully you'll still have enough for your phone calls.

They're not worth fighting, you think. *When they're adults, they'll still be here, and I'll be long gone.* You hope that, in the not-too-distant future, you'll be in Australia, maybe studying journalism.

Will Somalia ever be peaceful enough to go home to? you wonder. *Will I make it back there one day, when I'm an old man with a beard and grown-up children... and if I do, will it still feel like home?*

The thought of never being able to go back to your beautiful, troubled city by the ocean makes your heart ache.

You're lost in these thoughts until a man's voice, chanting passionately, breaks through them. There's something familiar about the voice. You're not sure yet where it's coming from. You listen more closely.

'The white imperialists took over our country,' intones the voice, 'but did the Somali people submit?'

'*No!*' comes a chorused response.

'Then the civil war tried to divide us along tribal lines, but did the Somali people submit?'

'*No!*' comes the chant again. It's getting louder.

You round a corner and see them: a small knot of twenty or so men, clustered around a man standing on a wooden box.

'And here we are, pushed out of our own country by foreign troops who refuse to let al-Shabaab take their rightful place as leaders – but will we submit?'

'*No!*' cry the men massed around the speaker.

Your blood seems to freeze. You've stumbled across a meeting of al-Shabaab supporters. You hide behind a woven thorn-tree fence and try to get a better look at the speaker's face. His voice is all too familiar.

The man has a long, gaunt face and a beard. One half of his face seems normal; his bright eye flashes and darts about the crowd. But the other half of his face is terribly disfigured. His other eye socket looks like a collapsed cave. His lips on the scarred half of his mouth are fused together in a hideous smile.

'We have to make sacrifices for our country,' he

says. 'As you see, I myself was injured in an attack that successfully killed a traitor Somali journalist.'

The crowd boos and hisses, and with a sickening blow, you realise who the speaker is. It's Qasim, the man who planted the bomb that killed Rahama. You thought he had also been killed in the explosion, but it seems that, instead, half of his face was ripped off and he survived. Then you notice that his robes hang limply at his side: the explosion also took an arm.

Good, you think savagely.

You are staring at Qasim with pure hatred when he suddenly looks up from his followers. You duck further behind the thorn tree fence, but it's too late. That one eye... that brown, fierce eye in that ravaged face... He saw you. He recognised you.

He pauses a moment in his speech before continuing. 'The first step,' he says clearly, and his voice carries a little further to where you are hiding, because, you can tell, he wants you to hear this, 'is to strengthen al-Shabaab's position in the camp by weeding out all traitors *and their relatives*.'

The crowd eagerly mutters approval. You start to run. Your breath and your limbs make a desperate, crashing rhythm. You tumble through the camp like a stone gathering speed downhill, shoving your way through crowds, beating the ground with your feet as if you want to kill the earth itself.

'Whoa whoa whoa whoa!' says Scavenger Jok, catching you by the shoulders as you charge towards home. 'What's the hurry, friend?' He sees that your cheeks are streaked with tears. 'Who's after you?'

'Arsenal,' you rasp, the breath still surging in and out of you. 'The bastard who killed my aunty. He's here. He saw me.'

'Okay,' says Jok. He is immediately businesslike. 'Let's get Jamilah, and come and stay with me tonight.'

Jok walks briskly to your tent with you to collect Jamilah. You leave your schoolbooks and your cooking pot behind in the tent, and only take Jamilah's blanket and the pen. Jok then guides you both back to his hut. He doesn't pressure you to explain yourself further. He just patiently takes Jamilah's hand in his, and answers her questions in a steady voice as you make your way to his home.

You're more certain than ever that you can trust Jok completely, and you blurt out the rest of your story to him as you walk – what happened to Aunty Rahama, her note, the pen, losing Aadan's phone number, why you had to flee from home, how Sampson helped you as best he could...

When you reach Jok's hut, there is a white woman

waiting outside. Her cheeks are bright pink with the heat, and she is wearing a shirt and long pants. She's a little fat.

'Hi!' she says brightly in English, and she gives an awkward wave as you approach.

Your mind reels. Is she here because she's heard you're in danger from al-Shabaab? No, surely not.

'Hello, I'm Mel-ah-nee,' she says clearly and slowly. She puts her right hand out to shake Jok's. 'I'm from the...' She stops when she sees that Jok has no right hand, just a stump. He offers her his left hand instead. She seems to wither on the spot.

The furious pounding in your heart from seeing Qasim slows down a bit. You almost want to chuckle.

'Goodness me. Um, I'm sorry.' She clears her throat. 'Do *you* speak *English*?'

'Yes, and Arabic, Dinka and a little Swahili,' says Jok politely, in English.

'Ah,' says Mel-ah-nee. 'Wonderful. I wish I could speak so many languages. Well, I'm here because I believe you make these wonderful bottle-lights?'

She gestures around Jok's neighbourhood. Nearly everyone here has one of your bottle-lights now.

'He invented them,' says Jok proudly, nodding to you.

You try to stand up straighter and look like an inventor, not someone who's just had stones thrown at him by bullies and been scared half to death by al-Shabaab. This is an opportunity, you're almost sure of it. You just have to work out how to use it.

'That's so impressive,' says Melanie warmly. 'They're so simple and useful!' She smiles broadly.

Melanie's the first white person you've ever met, and it's strange. You always thought these people drove around in jeeps and told refugees like you what to do. But this one seems so unsure and soft. You think she's kind of cute, like a puppy.

'Would you like a job for our organisation, teaching other people how to make these?' she asks. 'We'd like to see them used all over Dadaab.'

Jok invites her inside to look at his bottle-light and talk about how you install them. But while he's explaining, and Adut is making tea, you interrupt.

'My life is in danger from al-Shabaab! Terrorists,' you add, in case she hasn't heard of them. 'They killed my aunty and they're going to kill me and my sister!'

Melanie looks taken aback. 'Well, I've only just arrived in Dadaab, but if you're looking for protection, there's a secure UNHCR compound I could take you to—'

'Does your organisation have a computer? And a phone?' you demand.

'Yes, of course,' she begins, but Jok sees where you're heading with this plan and butts in.

'Then please, if you want our cooperation with your project, you must help this boy track down his uncle in Australia!'

'Of course, of course,' Melanie says again. 'Anything I can do to help.'

She gives you and Jok a ride in her air-conditioned car. Jamilah waits behind with Adut, despite her furious protests.

Inside her office in a brightly painted, boxy building, Melanie helps you to use the internet to find the phone number of Sampson's shop in Eastleigh.

You press the numbers into the phone as quickly as you can, and then wait as slow seconds tick by, as the phone rings and rings.

Please answer, you think. *Come on, Sampson. Please!*

✳ To continue with the story, go to page 151.

ampson's warm, familiar voice on the other end of the line makes you want to cry.

'Good news!' he cries. 'Your uncle Aadan in Australia replied to my email, and he wants to help you. Wait, I have his number!'

You copy it down.

'Good luck, brave boy,' says Sampson. You can picture him beaming. '*Chujio hutenda mema, mabaya huliangukia.* You are like a sieve: although bad things fall upon you, you can do good. And please give your darling sister a kiss from Uncle Sammy.'

Now you have Aadan's phone number again! You've been waiting for this for so long – since the night you first left home, almost seven months ago. But you feel suddenly overwhelmed with nerves. Will Aadan really want to help you?

The thought of Australia has kept you going through all the bad times, and now it's your very last escape route from al-Shabaab. If it turns out that you won't be able to go, you might as well surrender and let the terrorists crush you.

With a shaking hand, you take a deep breath and call the number. You hear the ringtone chirruping like a distant bird calling from a foreign shore. You force yourself to breathe out. Your palms are clammy, and now your whole body is trembling.

Chirp, chirp. Chirp, chirp.

You wonder what Aadan is doing as his phone rings in his pocket or bag: driving a fancy car, or watching a movie on a big screen?

'Yeah?' comes a man's voice, thickened from sleep. He's speaking English. 'Who is it?'

'It's me,' you say in Somali, and your voice echoes down the line and bounces back to you: 'Me – me. Rahama's nephew – phew – phew.'

'You're alive!' shouts the voice, in Somali now. 'Thank God! Where are you?'

There's so much to say. Aadan hurls questions at you like missiles. You tell him everything, starting with what you saw on the day Rahama died.

Aadan becomes very quiet. Occasionally you hear him sniff as you tell your story, and you wonder if he's crying.

You tell him about the pen. The note. Al-Shabaab coming to your home. Crossing the border, meeting Sampson. The bank account and having to flee for Dadaab, and how now, despite all your efforts, al-Shabaab are here too, breathing down your neck, edging ever closer...

'I'm getting you and Jamilah out of there,' promises Aadan. 'Can you leave the camp? Tonight, if you can. It's not safe to stay another day. I have a friend in Nairobi: Abshir. I'll give you his address and send him money, and from there we'll work out how to get you out of Africa. He can care for you in the meantime. Get to Nairobi as soon as you can. Keep the pen safe if you can, but that's all you need to do – we'll do more to investigate Bright Dream together when you get to Australia. When you're safe.'

Jok is looking at you expectantly when you hang up the phone. Your hands are still shaking.

'Well?' he asks.

Aadan's last words are ringing in your ears: *when you get to Australia...*

He said *when*!

'I'm going to Australia,' you whisper.

Jok whoops and punches the air with his one good hand. You feel a squeeze in your heart – he's so genuinely happy for you, but you'll be leaving him behind.

You look at the address you've copied down for Abshir: it's in Eastleigh, Sampson's suburb! Your heart lifts at the thought of seeing him again.

That night, by the light of a kerosene lamp in Jok's hut, you, Jamilah, Jok and Adut try to work out how you and Jamilah are going to get back to Nairobi. Getting a truck-ride back in the same way you got here is out of the question – you don't know anyone in Dadaab with enough money to buy a ride.

Maybe an aid agency could help you, but that would be a slow process, waiting for funds to trickle through and permission to be granted for you to leave the camp – and now that al-Shabaab knows you're here, you just don't have that kind of time.

Even now, Jok is sitting with his back pressed up against the door in case anyone tries to barge in. Everyone in the tiny hut is alert and tense. Jamilah is chewing on her thumbnail.

'I wish we could help you,' says Jok.

'You've already helped so much,' you say. 'Maybe we could walk to Nairobi.'

'Through the desert?' cries Adut. 'No way. If the heat doesn't kill you, you'll be murdered by bandits or snatched away by lions!'

'Lions?' gasps Jamilah.

Adut nods. 'It happens to many of the children who walk out of Sudan,' she says gravely.

'But most of the people who live in Dadaab walked here,' you say, thinking of the thousands of famine victims pouring over the border from Somalia, Sudan, Ethiopia or even further. 'And we need to get out of here as soon as possible. Tonight, even.'

'But for every one of those who survived the walk here,' frets Adut, 'another lies dead in the desert.' A tear rolls down her cheek. 'Stay awhile longer, hide with us, and we'll do what we can to raise the money for your truck-fare.'

You look Jamilah squarely in the face. Whatever you decide to do now, the risk will be just as great – if not greater – for her. She needs to have a say. 'What do you think?' you ask her.

Jamilah's eyes meet yours, and you suddenly realise how much she's growing to look like Aunty Rahama. 'We're strong enough to do it,' she says. 'I'd rather face the desert than al-Shabaab.'

I love her so much, you think. *But there's nothing I can do now that won't put her life in danger.*

Adut sobs quietly in the background and Jok rubs his brow. 'It's your choice, kid,' he says.

✳ If you leave Dadaab tonight on foot, go to page 156.

✳ If you wait in Dadaab to try to raise money for a truck-ride to Nairobi, go to page 167.

'We have to go tonight,' you say, standing up.

You need to get walking now, in the dark, to cover as much distance as you can before stopping to rest in the heat of the day.

On top of that, refugees aren't allowed to leave Dadaab without permission, so you'll need to sneak away under cover of darkness. And it's best to be well away from here before al-Shabaab even gets a whisper of your plans.

Now Jok is crying, as well as Adut. They embrace you and Jamilah in turn.

You and Jamilah arrange a blanket over her shoulders, and a bag on your back holding the little food Jok has and as much water as you can carry.

You slip through the dark camp, heading for the outskirts where the shelters give way to the desert. You'll cut around from there in an arc to reach the dusty main road to Nairobi.

At night you can stay close to the road, but in the daytime you don't want to be found by robbers, terrorists, or the Kenyan police, so you'll have to hide in the desert to rest, or walk well away from the road.

'So long, Dadaab,' Jamilah whispers with conviction.

You remember when you arrived, nearly seven months ago, and thought it looked, from the distance, like a little toy town made from mud. Now you know that it is bigger, more awful, and yet more wonderful, than any other place you've known. As you walk towards the outskirts of the camp, you promise yourself to return one day, not to seek help but to give it, in some way.

You are so lost in thought that you don't realise there is someone following you through the camp. Jamilah notices, though. She tugs your hand.

'There's a man! Behind that tent!'

You turn in time to see a black shape slip behind a shelter made of branches and a ragged tarpaulin. You stop a moment and stay very still, your senses quivering. It must be al-Shabaab. Then you hear the *click* of a gun being loaded.

You grab Jamilah tightly and duck behind a thorn-tree fence. On your hands and knees, you creep forward until you can see around the corner.

The man has stepped out from behind the shelter. His face is covered by a scarf, and he holds a long black gun. He is looking the other way – he's not sure where you've gone.

'Stay there,' you hiss to Jamilah, and you charge at the man. Your bare feet are so light and fast on the sandy ground that he sees you only a moment before you crash into him. He loses his balance and, grabbing you with one hand, pulls you both to the ground.

You are above him, and you make a desperate grab for his gun, but he is too fast and throws you onto your back. You can see him reaching for his weapon.

Suddenly, faster than a cat, Jamilah leaps out from behind the concrete wall, sprints towards you, lets out a bloodcurdling battle cry, and kicks the side of the man's face with all her strength. Blood drips out of his gaping mouth, and he looks at her in astonishment.

You make use of his momentary distraction to grab his gun. He is swiping at Jamilah, but she dodges him nimbly. You manage to wrestle the gun away from him, and you point it at him.

The man rises to his feet, but Jamilah shouts, 'Get back down! Or my brother shoots.'

Looking warily from Jamilah to you, the al-Shabaab militant drops to his knees.

'Now leave us alone – *forever*,' says Jamilah fiercely.

You are still pointing the gun at the man. It's heavy, an AK-47, more than half Jamilah's height. You've never fired a gun before, but you will if you have to, you're certain of that now.

You back away. He stays where he is, kneeling in the dirt. When you are far enough away, you sling the gun over your bag and across your back by its strap. Then, taking Jamilah's hand, you jog the rest of the way out of Dadaab and into the desert, until the distant shelters are only just visible in the moonlight. By keeping the camp within view and to your left, you can make your way around to the main road.

You set a strong pace, feeling jumpy but good. Rahama's golden pen bounces lightly in your pocket. 'You're a warrior, you know that?' you say to Jamilah. 'Like the Queen of Sheba!'

'I want to be like Aunty Rahama,' says Jamilah earnestly.

You look across at her in the moonlight. She looks older: she holds her mouth seriously and her shoulders square. When did she grow up? All this time, she's been an adored but helpless kid to you, but now you are walking into the desert as equals. You could have died back there without her help.

'Me too,' you say. 'Aunty Rahama was my hero.'

You half expect Jamilah to start crying – after all, you feel a lump in your own throat – but she marches forward.

You reach the main road: two deep tyre tracks of sand, heading roughly west. Dawn breaks behind you, making your shadows long and thin on the road ahead. The sand still feels cold around the edges of your thongs.

You walk on for a couple more hours, until the sun is well above the horizon and starting to build heat. Most of the thorn trees close to Dadaab have been stripped of branches for shelters, fences and firewood, but you see a good bushy one in the distance.

'We'll walk to that tree,' you tell Jamilah, pointing, 'then stop and rest. If we can sleep for a while, we'll have more energy to walk during the night.'

The tree is a little way off the road, and it's a good place to rest. You both sip a little water, and then you make a shady cover by hanging your blanket from a low branch.

Occasionally, a truck roars past. You sit as still as possible while the air around you heats to a temperature so high you can hardly keep your eyes open. It's hard to rest when it feels like your skin is going to split from the heat.

You slip in and out of a muddle of sleep. Only

when the day cools into evening do you start to
think clearly again.

You and Jamilah eat a little of the thick, doughy
millet that Jok gave you. It's the only food you've
eaten all day – bland and heavy, enough to keep
you moving.

You don't know how many nights this will take.
The second night of walking already doesn't feel as
easy as the first. You might have ten nights ahead of
you like this, or twenty, or more if you get lost.

The gun is heavy and cumbersome to carry, so
you and Jamilah take turns. You don't want to leave
it behind – you might need it for self-defence, and if
you ever see an animal, you could try shooting and
cooking it. But the only signs of life so far have been
flies, which came out yesterday during the heat of the
day, and a single lizard you saw last night at dusk.

You walk through the night and the following
dawn and morning. The strap on one of your thongs
breaks, and Jamilah rips the hem off her dress to tie
it back onto your foot.

The days turn to nights, then back into days.
Occasionally, as you rest during the days, you hear
a roar of an engine passing on the road, but you
always choose resting places that keep you well
hidden, and you only walk by the road at night as

planned. The millet dwindles. Soon you are eating just a pinch of millet, and then nothing – just a few sips of water a day.

At first, to keep your minds focussed on other things, you would tell Jamilah to recite her alphabet as she walked along, or you sang a song together. Now you both barely have the energy to speak.

But for every one of those who survived the walk here, another lies dead in the desert, says Adut's voice in your memory.

The desert wants to eat you.

Each evening you look into Jamilah's face, see her red-rimmed eyes, the skin hanging from her cheekbones like dry cloth, her slack, exhausted mouth without even a drop of spit in it to swallow, and you know it's a mirror of your own.

One day, as the heat starts to build, you stumble towards a resting place you've spotted: some sticks in the ground with a tarpaulin strung over them, a makeshift humpy half-buried in sand. Someone else who made this journey must have left their shelter behind.

But when you stumble closer, you realise the traveller is still there. Or, some of her is. A pile of clothes and bones and a hank of brown hair is all that's left of her body.

Jamilah starts to choke with dry sobs. 'No. No! We can't rest here with a dead woman!'

'We have to,' you say forcefully. 'There's nowhere else.'

Feeling sick to the stomach, you move the woman's bones aside. You shudder as you sit down next to them, pulling Jamilah into the shelter with you.

A sandstorm howls through the desert that day, blotting out the sun, filling your nostrils and ear-holes with sand.

When the sandstorm finally passes, the cool weather of evening has arrived, but since you didn't get any rest you find that you can't stand up and keep going. Your legs shake when you try, and you fall back to the ground. You feel like a hollow boy, made of sticks and string.

*Waterwaterwaterwate*r, says your brain. But there is none left. Jamilah lays her head in your lap. Her eyelashes are coated in sand. A little scrap of breath – in, out, in – is the only difference between her and the traveller's pile of bones beside you.

That night, you are tormented by dreams and visions. Men from al-Shabaab take your gun and tie it around your throat. Your parents arrive and sob as they try to untie the gun, asking, *Did we die for this? For you to be collared like an animal?*

The bones rise up from the ground and assemble themselves into a woman. The flesh grows on her body, then withers and falls away, and the bleached bones tumble to the ground again and again in a tortuous rewinding dance.

Rahama appears from the desert, and she is angry with you. *You failure!* she shouts. *You're both going to die!* Then she starts hitting you, and you wake to discover you've been hitting yourself.

You want to cry, but there's nothing left. You want to howl, but instead you just look at the moon, hearing that scrap of breath slide in and out of you, even as you wait for it to stop.

When dawn arrives, you can't wake Jamilah. You shake her, and her head flops from side to side but her sand-encrusted eyes won't open. You put your ear to her chest. There is still a steady, quiet drumbeat in there.

You heave her over one of your shoulders and stand. You're not going to die beside this woman's bones, under this last hopeless shelter in the desert.

You stumble towards where you think the road lies. The sandstorm has made it impossible to tell where it is – but then you hear the roar of an engine. You fling yourself into its path.

For a moment you think the ute isn't going to stop, but it grinds to a halt right in front of you. As you take in its occupants, your heart begins to pound and you feel dizzy.

The driver wears reflective sunglasses and is swathed in the chequered scarves that al-Shabaab militants sometimes wear. He wears a loop of bullets around his chest. In the back of his truck is a cargo of soldiers dressed in camouflage. Some of them don't look much older than you.

Your truckload of 'saviours' is a truckload of al-Shabaab recruits and their unit commander. You took a gamble, and the people who've stopped for you, the first people you've seen in all these days, are the same ones who ripped you from your homeland and want to kill you.

You think about running away, but it's hopeless – you don't have the energy to run alone, let alone with Jamilah's unconscious body slung over your shoulder.

'Where are you going?' the driver growls in Somali.

'Nairobi,' you manage to answer.

'Give me that gun and I'll take you there,' he barks in his gravelly voice.

You look again at the group of soldiers in the

back of the ute. Their faces seem hard and closed. Nobody smiles or makes eye contact.

If you go back out into the desert, praying for another ride, you may not survive.

But hitching a ride with this truckload of enemies – and giving them your only weapon to boot – seems positively suicidal. What if they work out who you are, or whom you stole this gun from in the first place?

You wonder if, either way, this will be the last decision you ever make.

+ To take your chances in the desert and refuse the ride, go to page 172.
+ To accept the lift, go to page 174.

You sigh. 'I think Adut is right,' you say. 'Let's just stay here a little longer and see if we can raise a fare to Nairobi.'

Two children walking alone through the desert for such a huge distance would be food for the vultures before too long.

The four of you stay awake late into the night listing all the ways you could try to raise the money.

'You could call your Uncle Aadan back and ask him to send some money direct to Dadaab?'

'Or call Sampson, and ask *him* for money?'

'We could always keep the half of the gold pen with the memory stick attached, and sell the other half.'

'Could I leave school and take up full-time scavenging and bottle-light making with, Jok?'

'We could all go mostly without food for a couple of weeks, and sell the rations?'

'Why don't you become a rap star?'

'Or a famous soccer player?'

'I could marry the president's daughter!'

'We'd better find out which presidents have nice daughters.'

You are really going to miss Jok and Adut when you're gone.

JUST BEFORE DAWN, when you are nearly asleep, a shock of adrenaline runs through your veins and launches you wide awake. You sit still as a stone, trying to work out what woke you.

Was it a bad dream? Jamilah twitching? Jok muttering? No...there's someone outside the hut. You're sure of it.

Calm down, you tell yourself. *Of course there's someone outside the hut.* It's nearly dawn – it will just be someone going off early to work, or perhaps a guilty man sneaking home after a night of drinking moonshine liquor with his mates.

You decide, as a favour to Adut, to take the water drum to the bore-hole and fetch her some water before the household wakes up. She has been so kind to you, and you would like to show your gratitude. And besides, you need to get out of the hut – the air is musty and thick, like the air in the ruined theatre by the sea when Zayd told you his story, and you're feeling as jittery and trapped as you did then. It will be too dangerous for you to go out later, when the camp is properly awake, so now is your chance.

You sneak to the door and open it slowly. *Creak.* You need to open it wider to get the water drum out with you. *Creeeeak.*

Outside, you look left and right. Nobody. One or two stars are left shining as the night's ink drains from the lightening sky. The shadows are still deep and dark, and the air smells like smoke. The sandy track to the bore-hole is cold under your bare feet.

Whump! As you pass a tall thorn-tree fence, someone steps out from behind it and whips a sack down over your head.

You fight desperately, wriggling and kicking, but they are strong and your arms are pinned tight to your sides. Through the sack, a hand clamps your mouth firmly closed, so that you struggle to breathe and your screams come out as a 'Mmmmph!' through your nose.

You hear a hollow *thump* as you kick the plastic water drum where you dropped it, and feel yourself strike what you think is a leg. Then your legs are promptly kicked out from under you and you fall backwards, your body hitting the dirt.

Someone has their knees on your chest. They are still pressing down on your mouth, too, so that the back of your head is shoved hard against the sandy ground.

Someone else standing nearby starts to kick you, and your chest and sides are on fire. You can manage to suck in tiny cracks of air through your nose, but if you don't get a deep lungful of air soon, you'll pass out.

'Where is it?' you hear a voice hiss in Somali. 'Where is it?' Then: 'Stop kicking him and search him!'

The kicks stop, and a hand rummages through your left shorts pocket. You realise what they're after: the pen. If only you'd left it in Jok's hut. But you know it's in your right pocket, and soon, so will they.

After they find it, they will kill me, you think. You just hope that they do it quickly, and somewhere private. Not in front of Jok, Adut or – Allah help her – Jamilah.

'*Yes!*' cries a second voice, and you feel the pen slide from your pocket like a dagger. 'Here it is!'

With the hand still over your mouth, your lungs are burning and you can't speak. If you could, though, you wouldn't use your breath to plead for mercy – you've seen enough of al-Shabaab to know that would be a waste. Instead, you'd use it to speak to Allah.

I've been faithful, you'd say. *Weigh my heart, look at it. See if the light shines through it. If you can't give me any more time on earth, then please, take me to be with my aunty again.*

You can't say the words, but you think them, and you wonder if something beyond the desert sky hears you.

Then dawn breaks, a single shot fires and, like an eagle flying over the Nile and out to sea, you are gone.

THE END

✦ To return to your last choice and try again, go to page 155.

You shake your head, and back away. You won't climb into a truck full of the very people you're running from.

The driver shrugs, revs his engine and roars off in a cloud of dust. You're lucky he didn't take the gun from you by force, or kill you both on the spot for not giving it to him. He must have had bigger fish to fry today.

You look back at the shelter with the woman's bones. You know with grim certainty that if you lie down in there again, you'll never get up. You'll have to stay beside the road, walk a little further if you can, and pray for another vehicle to pass soon.

You stagger onwards. Jamilah's lighter to carry than a girl her age should be, but she still feels too heavy for you to carry. You place one foot in front of the other, willing yourself on. *Just a little further, just … a little …*

Your knees collapse under you, and Jamilah's weight knocks you to the ground. You manage to roll her off you, then, by propping the gun upright in the sand and draping your two tattered blankets over it, you make a tiny hot triangle of shade.

Your eyes slide closed, and you feel yourself rippling like a heat haze, dissolving into the ever after. Your body, entwined with Jamilah's, lies unmoving, to be slowly buried by the weather, shipwrecked on a sandy sea.

THE END

✦ To return to your last choice and try again, go to page 166.

You nod your agreement. The driver holds out his arm, and you hand the gun to him through the ute's window.

Then you limp around to the back and pass Jamilah up to the soldiers sitting on two benches lining the sides of the ute's open tray, their knees meeting in the centre. By shifting their feet, they make space for you both on the floor.

Jamilah remains unconscious, lying at the soldiers' feet, and you sit behind her, your knees up and your arms folded tight around them. The ute revs forward along the sandy road. You push one of your blankets under Jamilah's head to keep it from banging against the floor of the truck and the soldier's boots.

At first, you don't speak to the soldiers. You merely watch them, and remain on your guard. But when one of them takes a sip from a water bottle, he looks down sideways at you and sees the thirst on your face.

'Here, have some,' he says, pushing the bottle towards you.

You eye him warily, but you can't refuse. You're

about to raise the bottle to your mouth when you think of Jamilah.

'Can you help me hold my sister's head up while I tip a little water in?' you ask.

The soldier nods. He reaches down, scoops up Jamilah's head, and gently pushes on her jaw to open her mouth. The water you tip from the bottle trickles out the sides of her mouth and onto her clothes, but you think she might have swallowed a bit.

'Keep giving it to her,' says the soldier. 'Little sips at a time. And have some yourself too. I don't need it back. We'll be in Nairobi by lunchtime.'

'Thank you' isn't big enough to convey the gratitude you feel.

The soldier, who introduces himself as Hassan, keeps helping you to give Jamilah water. She's still not conscious, but she's swallowing better, and you know that with some water inside her she has a much greater chance at hanging on to life.

The trip is mostly silent, until, after a few more hours, Hassan asks you: 'So, why are you going to Nairobi?'

All eyes suddenly fall on you. You don't expect that Hassan's kindness will continue if you reveal that you're wanted by al-Shabaab.

'My uncle might be able to get me a job there,' you lie. 'Loading trucks.'

Hassan nods. 'Lucky you. An uncle, and a job – that's more than most have.'

'I guess so.' You shrug. 'But we nearly didn't make it.'

Hassan smiles, but it's a sad smile. 'We all have our fates,' he says quietly. 'Yours must have been to live. Allah will decide ours soon enough. Hopefully he'll take mercy on a group of orphans.'

Orphans? You look around at the other boys in the back of the ute. Some of them are glaring at Hassan, as though he's said too much. Others share his sad, resigned smile.

'We're orphans too,' you tell them, hoping to gain their trust.

'Then you were lucky to escape Bright Dream,' whispers Hassan.

Your heart leaps at that name, but the boy-soldier next to Hassan immediately snaps, 'Shut up! Don't talk about it!'

'I will if I want to,' persists Hassan. 'After all, you have to tell the truth before you die if you want to enter Paradise...'

The soldier next to Hassan growls and rolls his eyes, but Hassan leans forward to talk to you.

'We're all from Bright Dream,' he mutters, so low that only you can hear him above the roar of the engine. 'Al-Shabaab runs it. Our families died in the war, and the orphanage claimed us, then trained us to be soldiers. It's more like a farm than an orphanage – where boys are raised to die in their war.'

You wonder what kind of mission has brought them into Kenya, but you don't dare ask. You think of Bright Dream's bank account, the figures in their millions spooling down Sampson's computer screen – all supposedly spent on boys like Hassan. You wonder if it's gun money, money stolen by al-Shabaab...or if it's been donated by unwitting foreign donors, hoping to help the poor.

Either way, it's the perfect plan for al-Shabaab, you think. An organisation like theirs would take a lot of money to run, and a lot of soldiers to fight for them. Bright Dream can provide both, without arousing suspicion.

You realise suddenly that exposing Bright Dream isn't just about taking al-Shabaab down – it's also the only way to save countless boys like Hassan from their fate.

The ute jerks to a halt and you are nearly thrown to the floor. You sit back up, alarmed. You are still in the middle of the desert. The driver gets out and stamps around to the back where you all sit. His mirrored sunglasses give nothing away.

'What are you talking to the boy about?' he barks at Hassan.

He must have been watching Hassan talk to you in the rear-view mirror. Hassan straightens up guiltily. You realise that this man has the same job Zayd once did – training boys, sending them to fight, then killing them if they were of no more use.

You think fast. 'We're from the same clan, sir. He was asking if I knew his deceased family at all, sir.'

'*Nobody* talks to the boy! Or his sister!' shouts the man in a fury, ignoring the fact that Jamilah is still unconscious. 'The next person who talks will be shot!'

Some of the boy-soldiers give Hassan accusing glares, as if to say *thanks a lot*.

The driver gets back into the cabin and starts driving again. Hassan shrugs and purses his lips. For the rest of the trip, he obeys the order not to speak. He shakes his head when you look at him expectantly – it's clear you can't ask him any more questions. But he still helps Jamilah to take mouthfuls of water.

You are leaving the desert now and coming into farmland. Brightly dressed women walk here and there with bundles on their heads, and you see a boy with a stick herding cattle, while younger children play hopscotch in the dirt. You can smell cow dung and cooking fires getting ready for lunch.

You lift Jamilah's head for another sip of water and she stirs. Then her eyelids flutter. Your heart leaps, and you beg Allah for her to open her eyes. She does. Her brown eyes lock onto yours and crinkle as she smiles.

Relief floods through you like a king tide. You squeeze her bony shoulders.

Thank you, thank you, thank you! you want to shout to the world. For Hassan and his water; for Allah's mercy. You can't stop the tears coming to your eyes. She sits up and you wrap her in a hug that you never want to end.

Jamilah looks around then, at the truck and the soldiers, and you see her eyes widen in fear. She has no idea where you are or who these people are.

You hug her again and whisper into her ear: 'It's okay. But shhh!'

A tired, relieved smile washes over Jamilah's face. Then she nestles her head against your chest and sleeps peacefully all the way to Nairobi.

WHEN YOU REACH the outskirts of Nairobi, you crawl to the front of the ute tray and rap on the driver's window.

'Eastleigh?' you shout, and you see him nod.

After driving through the city for a while longer, he stops the truck and shouts: 'This is Eastleigh,' from inside the cabin.

You give Hassan a tiny smile in farewell – it's all you dare to do. You hope he understands how grateful you are for his kindness. You try not to imagine what his future will hold.

You are in a busy street, lined with shops and restaurants. The smell of meaty stew makes your mouth water. The apartment belonging to Aadan's old friend Abshir, who is taking you in, is somewhere around here. You've memorised the address – but you wait until the ute has long driven away before you ask a shopkeeper for directions. You don't want the ute-driver knowing where you're heading, or remembering you for anything other than giving him your gun in exchange for a ride.

Equipped with directions, you and Jamilah stagger through the tall columns of apartment blocks, Jamilah's arm slung over your shoulders for support.

People stare at you curiously. Some of them look

afraid. You look down at your body – it's like a piece of rusty wire dressed in rags. But you battle onwards. Every step you take, you think, *We did it. We made it out of the desert, alive.* You're proud of your wire-and-rags body. Next stop: Australia.

You find Abshir's apartment block. With your final burst of strength, you and Jamilah manage to climb seven flights of stairs and rap on the wire security door of his apartment.

A young guy with a white shirt and masses of curly hair opens the door, and before you even introduce yourself, he drops to his knees so he's eye-to-eye with Jamilah.

'Whoa!' he exclaims. 'Are you Aadan's niece and nephew?'

You nod, and he embraces you both so tightly you nearly lose your balance.

'Oh, you beautiful kids, what on earth *happened* to you? Aadan called me, you didn't show up for a week, then he says he thinks you tried to *walk* here! Get in here right now, I'm going to make you fatter than a pair of baby hippos! And then I'm going to call your uncle – he was just about to hop on a plane and come look for you himself!'

Inside, you look around Abshir's lounge room in wonder. A music video is playing on a large TV.

Abshir gives you just some plain biscuits with milk at first, as your stomachs aren't used to food.

'Don't scoff them too quickly, walaal, or you'll vomit!' he cries.

You smile. 'Walaal' is Somali for 'friend', and you know you've found a good one in Abshir.

'This is better than a movie star's mansion,' enthuses Jamilah, and Abshir laughs, but you totally agree.

Half an hour later, you are standing in Abshir's shower. Warm water pours over your skin. Even back home in Mogadishu, you only washed with a cold tap and bucket. This is a miracle. Taps! Lights! Warm water! Soap! You open your mouth and swallow the water as it cascades over your face.

You can hear Abshir talking to Aadan in the next room: 'They're alive…an absolute miracle, walaal, praise Allah…I know, I would have paid for them too if I'd known, but it sounds like they had to get out of there in a hurry…I know you're worried, but they're safe here – no one from Arsenal knows they're here…They can't talk right now – your niece is asleep on my lap and your nephew's in the shower – but we'll call again soon…You're going to love them so much, I swear, they're just amazing…'

You lie down that night on soft sheets, and before

you can even whisper goodnight to Jamilah, you're both fast asleep.

The days after that pass in a blur. At first, your stomach aches when you eat any food at all, even though you want to stuff your face. You and Jamilah spend a lot of time sleeping as your bodies slowly get stronger again, while Abshir goes out to work for a phone company in downtown Nairobi.

You and Jamilah talk to Aadan on the phone, and although it's only the second time, he feels like family to you already.

'Abshir and I are making a plan to get you guys to Australia,' he promises. 'There's nothing more important to me in the world right now than making sure you're safe. I spent all day at the embassy today – it might take a while, but we'll work something out.'

You call Sampson too, who can't wait to see you both. You tell him how much you want to let Adut and Jok know you made it here safely, and it turns out he's recently met a businessman who takes loads of tinned food to sell in Bosnia regularly, who could pass along the message.

Abshir, who's listening in, promises to take you to meet with Sampson at a nearby coffee shop the next day – it's only a few blocks away, so it seems like a safe enough excursion. You are all delighted.

'Everything's working out just great!' laughs Jamilah once you've hung up.

'Jamilah,' you say warningly, 'I know it feels like our new life in Australia is just around the corner, but remember how everyone checked the resettlement noticeboard in Dadaab every single day – visas to Australia are rare as hen's teeth. We still might be holed up here, hiding, for a year or two, maybe more.'

'It's still better than we've ever had it since we left home,' Jamilah insists, and she's right.

'Getting you visas is going to be damn hard,' admits Abshir. 'You don't have passports, and even if you did, the Australian government would make you wait years for visas. Your uncle's even talking about adopting you, but man, *that's* more complicated than a basketful of snakes. Uncle Aadan's going to send some money for me to look after you here in the meantime, don't worry. Although I am sorry you won't be able to go to school, or out much at all.'

'That's okay,' you say. 'Thank you very much for having us.' Your heart is glowing to imagine being Aadan's legally adopted kids, no matter how long it takes.

'Walaal, it's no problem at all,' replies Abshir.

A thought occurs to you. In Dadaab, you sometimes heard stories of people who tried to reach a safe country in the same way that you crossed the border from Somalia into Kenya: undercover, without papers. 'Could we get to Australia without a visa?' you ask. 'Maybe hiding in trucks or boats?'

Abshir grins. 'Oh, walaal, you and your sister – I've never met such a tough pair of kids. You just walked through the desert, and now you're ready to take on a journey like that? Look, it can be done, but I don't think it's safe, and nor does your Uncle Aadan. Especially not alone. Let's just chill and stay safe in old Eastleigh for now, okay?'

True to his word, Abshir takes you and Jamilah to meet Sampson the next afternoon. Sampson leaps up from his seat when he sees you and rushes to embrace you both. Then he loads your pockets with sweets he's brought from his shop.

'Oh, children, I've had so many sleepless nights worrying for your safety!' he cries. 'It's sweeter than honey to see you again. *Hakuna kilicho kitamu kuliko kilichopatikana kwa shida*. There is nothing sweeter than what has been obtained at great effort. Am I right?'

You grin so much that your cheeks hurt. He

strokes Jamilah's head and she closes her eyes in bliss.

It's dark by the time you all finally say farewell and leave for home. Abshir is half a flight ahead of you as you climb the stairs to his apartment; you're helping Jamilah, who still tires very easily. Then Abshir's usually cheerful voice echoes back down from the internal door at the top of the stairwell, sounding stunned: 'Whoa. Kids, *stop*. Don't move a muscle.'

You both glance up in alarm, to see him turn in the open doorway and look down at you. His eyes are wide. 'Now, don't panic,' he says quietly, 'but I want you to stay down there, all right? No matter what you hear. If someone comes after you then *run*.'

He closes the stairwell door leading to the seventh-floor corridor behind him, and you and Jamilah stand staring at each other in a hollow silence.

You can hear the fluorescent lights in the stairwell buzzing, and Jamilah's quick breaths. *What now?* you think. *Why us? Can't we be safe and happy for more than a few days at a time?*

You realise that you can't leave Abshir to face whatever this is alone – especially if you're somehow the cause of it. Dreading what you will find, you take Jamilah's hand and climb the last stairs, then open the door to the corridor.

The metal security door to Abshir's apartment has been busted off its hinges. All the doors of your neighbours remain closed and silent, bearing no witness. Entering the dark apartment nervously, you see Abshir standing in the middle of his wrecked home.

'They're gone,' he whispers hollowly as you walk in. 'At least they didn't stay to do damage to us.'

Shattered glass from the windows makes the floor sparkle in the moonlight. The TV screen is a buckled cobweb of cracks; the table is upside down; even the curtains are ripped from their rail.

You look at the wall, at the red writing sprayed there, and you know who did this: the same people who have wrecked your life, your country, and your family since the day you were born.

'GIVE US THE PEN.'

It's al-Shabaab.

You don't know how they found you here – did the guys from the ute hear about the two escaped kids, and follow you after they dropped you off in Eastleigh? Did Sampson's business contact who was passing the message on to Jok let something slip?

Or had al-Shabaab tapped the phone you used in the camp?

Right now, you don't even care – you're ready to crack from the pressure of needing to run away, again and again and again. Jamilah is silent as a stone. You feel like howling. You scrunch up your fists, press them into your eye sockets, and moan.

Abshir's hand on your shoulder makes you stop. You pull the pen from your pocket and look at it. Its ruby tip has never seemed more like a drop of blood. Having it has always made you feel like a hero, but right now it feels like nothing more than a curse – a magnet for death.

'What if we give it to them?' you ask desperately. 'If we give Arsenal what they want, will they leave us in peace?'

'No, we can't do that!' Jamilah cries. 'Aunty Rahama trusted us with it!'

'But Jamilah, what's the point in trying to uncover Bright Dream? We're just two kids. Al-Shabaab is everywhere.'

The bitter unfairness of it rises up to overwhelm you. 'I'm just so sick of it!' you shout, kicking the torn, upended couch. 'They ruin *everything*! What do we have to do to get rid of them?'

Abshir stands in the centre of his smashed-up

apartment like a rock at sea. 'I think, walaal,' he says slowly at last, 'that maybe – just maybe – if you give them the pen, they might leave you in peace. Or...' – he seems to be thinking through his next words carefully before speaking – 'if you *do* decide to keep that pen, you're going to have to take it far, far away.'

You know, with sickening certainty, that he's right.

* To give al-Shabaab the pen and stay with Abshir, waiting for safe passage to Australia, go to page 203.
* To keep the pen and risk trying to reach Australia without papers, go to page 190.
* To read a fact file on people smugglers, turn to page 317, then return to this page to make your choice.

You look at the pen in your hand and the words from Rahama's letter come back to you: *This pen really means so much to me. In the darkest of times, it's given me hope that freedom does exist. Now I pass it on to you, because there is no one else I know in the world with such an enquiring mind and fearless heart... You are a special boy. Take this pen, and with Aadan's help, finish what I couldn't.*

You can't surrender your freedom. You can't hand over the truth that Aunty Rahama died for. You'll keep the pen, no matter what the risks. You'll take it as far away from here as you can.

'Okay,' you say to Abshir. 'Do you have a walaal who can get us to Australia?'

Jamilah grins and squeezes your hand. 'We can do it,' she whispers to you. You don't know how she manages to stay so determined, but you love her for it.

In the midst of all the mess in his smashed apartment, Abshir starts making phone calls.

A few hours later, he says: 'All right! I've found

a walaal who knows a walaal who can talk to his walaal.'

He grins, winks. Then his expression becomes serious.

'But I don't think we should tell Aadan. He'll lose it. You know he loved your Aunty Rahama more than all the love songs in the world. He'll flip his lid if he finds out we're under attack and I'm giving you to a people smuggler.'

There is a long silence as his words sink in.

'Can you handle this alone?' he asks, with tender concern.

You look at Jamilah. She puts her hands on her hips and fixes you with a determined glare you think she's inherited from your aunty. 'We're going,' she says.

YOU LEAVE THE wrecked apartment – it's too dangerous to stay there another moment.

'I'll pay for the damage and find somewhere else to live after I have you kids sorted,' Abshir assures you. 'For now, we're going into hiding.'

He takes you to a dirty, ramshackle house in an alleyway, where a chain-smoking Kenyan guy in a white singlet lets you rent a stuffy room in his attic.

The next day, a Somali man with one grey tooth comes and drinks coffee with Abshir while they haggle over prices to smuggle you to Australia. You listen in, and you're horrified – it's enough money to buy a car, or to set up a small business.

Two days later, Grey Tooth comes back with forged travel documents for you and Jamilah, and Abshir hands him an envelope stuffed with cash.

'Where did you get the money?' you ask Abshir. 'Is it all of what Aadan sent you to look after us for a whole year?'

'Yep, just about, walaal,' he says and sighs. 'He'll want the same amount again once you arrive safely – what I gave him today is only half the cost. But I'll worry about that. Now listen here.'

Abshir reaches into a plastic bag and takes out a pair of new blue sneakers in just your size. He lifts up the sole of one, takes some unfamiliar green notes out of his pocket, and stashes them under the sole.

'That's five hundred US dollars, walaal – more money than I make in a month, all right? It has to last you the whole journey – from here by plane to Malaysia, then by boat to Indonesia, and finally another boat to Australia. The whole journey is paid for, and there'll be someone to meet you at each place, so don't give the smugglers anything extra. The cash is mostly in case you need to bribe a border official, but also in case you need to pay for food or get a local simcard for the phone.'

Next, he hands you a new phone. You can scarcely believe your eyes.

'This, walaal, is courtesy of my work,' he says and chuckles. 'Proud sponsor of Screw You, Al-Shabaab.'

You both laugh.

AS YOU FOLLOW Abshir through Nairobi airport, tightly holding Jamilah's hand, your new blue sneakers make a little *eek*, *eek*, *eek* on the shiny floor.

When it's time to go, you embrace Abshir with all your strength, until he laughs and gasps for breath. 'Good luck, my little walaal' are his last words to you before you and Jamilah leave Africa…maybe forever.

On the plane, the engine roars. The pressure of the take-off glues your back to the seat. Jamilah's eyes grow wide as two coins. You have to jam your hands between your legs to stop them from shaking. You're suddenly so nervous that it feels like your guts are trying to ride down a mountain on a one-wheeled bike.

You look out the window at the desert unfolding below you. A few weeks ago, you and Jamilah were specks in that desert, a hair's breadth from death. You take some slow breaths and turn your attention away from the window.

The hours begin to tick by. So, this is what it's like to be on a plane. There are headphones and blankets for free, movies to choose from in different languages, portions of food wrapped in crisp plastic, and a tiny bathroom with a toilet that sounds like a blowtorch when you flush it.

An English word you've never heard before, 'turbulence', is announced, and then – *whoa!* – the plane dips and lurches and you feel like food tossed about in a frying pan.

The plane straightens up, and after a while Jamilah falls asleep. Her shoulders shake as she coughs in her sleep, and you try – and fail – not to think about how completely she's relying on you to get her through this journey.

But I'm relying on her too, you think. *I couldn't face this alone.*

You don't want to think about what could go wrong if the deal Abshir has helped you make goes bad and you get stranded in another country halfway to Australia. Abshir warned you that the

Malaysian and Indonesian governments are just as merciless to asylum seekers as the Kenyan police.

You make yourself think about going to school in Australia instead. About meeting Aadan; helping him write articles about al-Shabaab and Bright Dream, making sure Zayd and Rahama didn't die in vain. About getting Jamilah strong and healthy again, in a place where she can eat good food and see great doctors, and where both of you can even play sport, on a big grassy field, without al-Shabaab forbidding sport, and music, and education for girls, and drawing pictures, and all the other crazy things they forbid. You think about starting a new life in a place where you can be free.

The plane touches down in Kuala Lumpur, Malaysia. You and Jamilah stagger off the flight. Uniformed guards stand everywhere, and you feel waves of nervous nausea begin to wash over you.

You try to arrange your face to look nonchalant, as though you travel all the time, as though you have family waiting for you on the other side of customs.

'Just relax,' you hiss to Jamilah, and she nods tensely.

You force your feet onwards to the customs counter and lift your and Jamilah's forged papers up to the counter. The uniformed woman looks at them. She looks at you, then Jamilah. An eternity hangs in the air. She flips the paper over and sighs through her nose.

You're reaching down to untie your shoe – you hadn't thought about how clumsy it would be to get the bribe money out in public. You feel exposed as a snail without a shell. Then she gives a bored harrumph, and her stamp goes *chomp* on your paper, then *chomp* on Jamilah's.

'Okay,' she says, gesturing you onwards, and you're through.

A squat, balding Malaysian man with sweat patches under the sleeves of his shirt grabs you from the crowd, quickly checks your names, and hustles you into the back of his silver car.

He accelerates away from the airport, not speaking at all. On the car's radio, a woman's voice sings a high-pitched, lilting melody.

The air here is hot and wet. Green leaves and vines drip from every roadside, curling around fences, posts and anything else that stands still long enough for them to grow on. Billboards advertise noodles and new apartment blocks with swimming pools. The traffic moves fast and smooth.

It's like no other place you've ever been. The only thing that reminds you of home is one stray, spotty dog you see walking beside the highway. He is bony and grinning, and he looks like a survivor. His face is the only one here so far that has said to you: *You can do this.*

The people smuggler, who you decide you'll secretly call Piggy, parks on a crowded street. Then he takes you and Jamilah inside a crumbling stone building that might once have been a grand old home, but now seems to have been converted into some sort of boarding-house.

The space is crowded with bunks, cardboard boxes and plastic plants, but you don't see anyone else there. Piggy leads you down a flight of stairs into a basement room, which holds a double bed with a maroon cover, a TV and an ashtray loaded with butts, some with lipstick on them.

Piggy thrusts a plastic bag at you, containing bottled water and colourful plastic packets of chips and biscuits. Then he leaves, and locks the door behind you – still without having said a word.

You don't know how long you'll be here – Abshir only said that Grey Tooth had lined up all the transfers. You are now effectively Piggy's prisoners. You want to call Abshir, but you didn't get to ask Piggy for a Malaysian simcard.

You and Jamilah watch Malaysian TV and eat

chips with a strange cheesy-fishy flavour. Jamilah's cough seems to be getting worse. You touch her forehead.

'You're burning up!' you gasp.

You give her your share of the bottled water and encourage her to keep drinking.

You both try to get to sleep, but Jamilah wakes in the night moaning. Her body shivers all over, and she is doubled up with pain.

'What is it?' you ask her. 'What hurts?'

'My joints ache,' she whimpers. 'My head is pounding.'

You sit up and put your arm around her. Then you watch the BBC news channel while you pray for her fever to get better. The world news shows that the famine in Somalia is getting worse, fighting has broken out in Mali, and protestors are choking the streets of Egypt.

You want a glimpse of home, but all you see are ravaged lands in the countryside and black faces of despair. This isn't *your* Africa. Is this what the rest of the world sees when they look at your home?

You nod off, but Jamilah's gasp wakes you. She's pointing at the TV.

'Aunty Rahama!' she cries.

'Jamilah, whaaa—'

'It was her! I saw her! It was Aunty Rahama on the TV!'

You touch her forehead. Still hot. She might be hallucinating. But you look at the TV, still on the BBC news channel, and it's showing a segment about refugees arriving in Italy – desperate people, drenched in salt water, wearing orange lifejackets, being hauled aboard a coastguard's boat.

You search the faces. No Rahama.

'Jamilah, you must have seen someone who looks like her, that's all.'

'It was *her*!' Jamilah cries with all her strength, then doubles over coughing.

You're about to say, 'Let's switch it off,' when you see an image that makes you just about jump out of your skin.

'*Zayd!*' you gasp. You leap off the bed and run to the TV, as if you can cross through the glass screen and jump aboard that boat.

Now your heart is hammering like a rattling engine. You only got a glimpse, but you *know* that you saw the face of Zayd. You remember again his shout as al-Shabaab dragged him away to be killed: *Cross the river on the banner of the eagle!*

What if he *wasn't* killed? What if he escaped? What if he's now in Europe, with … *Rahama*?

But how could that be? You saw the bomb that destroyed the broadcast building, and her scarf at the window ... and, no, she would never leave you and Jamilah alone like that, not without even telling you where she'd gone. You watch the news segment to the end regardless, but there is no more sign of Zayd or Rahama.

'It can't have been her,' you say to Jamilah. 'It can't have been *him*, and it certainly can't have been her ...'

You just can't get your head around what it would mean if it really was her.

'It was!' Jamilah sobs. 'I promise, it *was*!'

She coughs again, her skinny body heaving, like a blanket when you shake the dirt off it. Then she stops. She's looking at her hand, where she coughed. She looks worried.

You look at her hand too, and with horror see that she's coughed up blood.

You run to the door. It's locked. You hammer on it. 'Help!' you shout in English.

After a couple of minutes of shouting, Piggy comes to the door. He looks sleepy and cross.

'No shout,' he tells you in English. 'You shout and police hear, they come and take you jail. Understand?'

'Yes, I understand,' you say. 'But my sister...she's very sick.'

Piggy comes into the room. He touches Jamilah's burning head, sees the spots of blood on her hand and the sheets. Then he shrugs and shakes his head.

'No doctor, no hospital in Malaysia for refugees,' he tells you. 'Only for Malaysians.'

'I know,' you say, boiling with frustration. Couldn't he be more helpful?

You're just about to offer him some of your stash of money to buy medicine when Jamilah shouts in English: 'Take me and my brother to Europe! Please! We want to go to Italy!'

'What?' says Piggy. 'You go Australia.'

'No,' insists Jamilah, sitting on the bed fighting for breath, tears running down her face. 'We saw our aunty in Italy, on TV. You send us to Italy!'

Piggy's eyes narrow. 'Huh,' he says. 'Maybe is possible. Many people here go to Europe. But is expensive. Five hundred more.'

Jamilah looks at you. 'I promise,' she whispers. 'It was *her*. Just trust me!' Then she starts to cough again.

You have five hundred dollars. You might even be able to bargain Piggy down a bit, so you can still buy the medicine for Jamilah.

Italy... You know even less about that country than you do about Australia. But it would be a safe place – you just saw the news segment about refugees being saved from the sea and cared for there. You're certain that Zayd is there. Is it possible that Rahama's there too?

Will you risk everything to find out?

✷ If you offer Piggy your money to send you to Italy, go to page 216

✷ If you stick with the plan to go to Australia, turn to page 209.

You keep gazing at the pen, and the longer you look at it, the more you see that it has become the source of all your misfortune. It's the reason your aunty's dead; the reason you've never been safe since, not in any of the places you've tried to make home. Why haven't you considered getting rid of it before now?

'If you're going to give them the pen,' says Abshir, 'I think we should copy the information on it first. We can email it to Aadan. I should have done it as soon as you got here, I was just so busy looking after you—'

'Can you *do* that?' you splutter.

'Of course, walaal! You don't know much about computers, do you?'

'So, I can give them the pen – they'll leave me alone – but we don't have to lose Aunty Rahama's story?'

'Exactly.'

It's the perfect solution – so long as the al-Shabaab terrorists believe you really have handed over the last copy in existence. You cling to the belief that it's possible.

You pause, then ask Abshir: 'But how will we get the pen to them?'

'I think,' replies Abshir, 'we just need to wait here.'

He takes the pen from you, and unlocks the drawer where, thankfully, his laptop lies untouched.

ABSHIR HAS SENT the email, and the three of you have cleared up the worst of the damage and are taking turns trying to sleep on the couch, when at two o'clock in the morning you hear a group of people coming up the stairwell.

The three of you hold hands tightly and wait. You're unarmed and unprotected, because you don't want to give them any reason to start a fight. You couldn't close the busted door even if you wanted to.

Fear rises in your stomach like a cold flood.

Take the pen and go, you think in a fast-repeating loop, *take the pen and go*.

Your palms are damp with sweat. One hand holds Jamilah's, the other holds the pen.

Five men walk into the apartment. You recognise the driver from the ute in the desert. There are three more heavily muscled men and, lastly, looking at his feet…

'Hassan?' you gasp. *So it was them!* you think.

Hassan can't look at you. The ute-driver glares at him. You can see from Hassan's body language that he doesn't want to be here but has no choice.

You walk over to Hassan and put the pen in his hand.

'Take it,' you say. 'I don't want anything more to do with you guys. Just take it and leave us in peace.'

Hassan takes the pen, but he still won't meet your eye. You don't know why the men don't seem more pleased to have got what they wanted. Then you hear a squeal from behind you, and a shout from Abshir.

You whirl around. The ute-driver is holding Jamilah by the neck. Two of the muscled men push Abshir against a wall and pin him there.

'Let her go!' you shout, springing towards Jamilah, but the third muscled man grabs you too.

'She hasn't done anything wrong. She has nothing to do with this,' chokes Abshir.

'Oh, we know she doesn't,' replies the ute-driver in his gravelly voice. Is that the gun you gave him in the desert that's slung over his side? 'But she's valuable to us nonetheless. You see,' he goes on, 'it's nice of you to give us the pen, but how do we know you haven't copied the information?'

Your panic mounts.

'We haven't!' protests Abshir, but they seem to know he's lying. 'Check my computer!' he begs.

Tears are running down Jamilah's face and onto the ute-driver's arm. She is squirming futilely. *Please*, say her eyes. *Please*.

Your heart is jumping wildly, like it wants to break out of your ribcage. You fight against the muscled guy holding you, but he's too strong.

'No,' says the driver, 'we'll take this girl. We'll keep her with us. In a couple of years, she'll make a lovely wife. And if you ever, *ever* make the information on that pen public – if anyone at all comes sniffing around Bright Dream ever again – we will kill her.'

Jamilah lets out a loud sob of terror.

A volcano of rage explodes inside you, so powerful that your whole body is possessed with violent, superhuman energy. You thrash and twist like a blade of grass in a storm, and suddenly you're free of the muscly man holding you. You fling yourself at Jamilah as the driver drags her backwards out of the door.

Abshir is shouting, 'Stop! No! Take me instead!' and trying to punch the two men who are still pinning him to the wall. Hassan is shuffling towards the door.

'*Hassan!*' you scream, knowing he's your last hope, the weak link in the chain. '*Save her! Hassan!*'

Hassan finally meets your eye, and you see something awful there. First, a little boy looks out from his face – a little boy who tried so hard to be the good boy his parents believed he could be, before they were killed by the war and he lost everything. Then Hassan's face seems to close over. The little boy vanishes. His eyes go dead and narrow, his mouth pulls tight. He raises a gun at you, and the gun is shaking.

You keep looking him in the eye as he backs away towards the door.

A sob from Jamilah wrenches your eyes back to her, just as she disappears through the doorway and out of your sight.

You throw yourself towards her, and Hassan fires his gun. Pain rips through your leg and you drop to the floor. The two men holding Abshir punch him and throw him to the ground too, and as you both struggle to get up, they all vanish.

YOU DIDN'T KNOW there was something worse than dying, but now you do. The wound in your leg heals – you always wonder whether Hassan was being merciful or if it was just a bad shot – but the pain in your heart will never heal. Every day, awake and asleep, you little sister is in your mind.

Time passes. The first months are frantic and full of action, attempts to rescue her. Then action gives way to despair as it becomes clear that she will never be found.

Aadan still wants to bring you to Australia, but you refuse to go. You won't leave Jamilah behind to face a fate you were spared from. You won't leave Africa, the continent that made you, that made all the beautiful and terrible things you have ever known.

Like the desert dust, instead you drift back across the border into Somalia, never settling, always searching. For revenge. For clues. For a sign.

Like the dust, people try to get rid of you, but you find your way back, through corners and cracks. Like the dust, you are loose and dry, stripped of meaning, only looking for that one deep drink of water that will make you whole again, but which you will never find: your lost sister, Jamilah.

THE END

✦ To return to your last choice and try again, go to page 189.

'Look,' you say to Jamilah in Somali, 'even if you're right about Aunty Rahama, us trying to go to Italy is pointless. If she's alive, she'll find us – you know she will. Aadan will look after us in Australia. We can search for Aunty Rahama from there. And we need to make that money last, not give it all to Piggy.'

To Piggy, you say in English: 'No. We still want to go to Australia. Soon – we want to go this week. No waiting.'

Piggy looks from one of you to the other. He's clearly pissed off. 'Stupid kids. Wake me up with shouting.' He turns to go.

'Wait!' you cry, taking fifty dollars from your shoe. 'I know we can't see a doctor, but at least buy her some medicine. And a Malaysian simcard,' you add hastily, as he snatches the money.

'Shops closed now,' Piggy snaps. 'I get it tomorrow.'

You sit on the bed with your arms around Jamilah as she drifts into a feverish sleep. *A long time ago*, you think, *we lived in Mogadishu, and we were kids*.

You don't feel like you're a kid anymore. *Kids*

get to have adults who look after them and friends who play with them. You're not sure you can even remember how to play. *Can you ever go back to being a kid, once you've stopped?* you wonder. *Or is it a one-way door?*

The morning comes and goes. Mid-afternoon, Piggy comes in and throws a battered box of medicine at you.

'Wait!' you shout when you look inside the box, which says 'Panadol' on the front. All the tablets have been popped out and used except for the last two. 'That's not fifty dollars' worth of medicine! Get her some proper medicine! She needs—'

But the door is slammed in your face, and fifty dollars of your money is gone. You have no idea if he'll get you the simcard.

Seething with anger, you snap a tablet in half to try to make the medicine last longer and give it to Jamilah.

The Panadol does seem to bring down her fever, at least a little. But you never get the simcard. You know Abshir will be worried, and you wonder how long he'll keep lying to Aadan about where you really are.

The next morning, Piggy wakes you and Jamilah before dawn and drives you to the coast.

'You go to Indonesia on fishing boat,' he says, pointing to where a blue wooden boat sits waiting in the mangrove shallows. 'In Indonesia, man will meet you. Then get on boat to Australia. Okay?'

You nod. Piggy says something in Malaysian to the fisherman, a wiry man dressed in a singlet and a chequered sarong, who lifts up the deck of his boat. Inside the hull is a splintery, damp hole just big enough to lie down in. It smells of fish guts and mud.

'We nail you in here, okay?' says Piggy.

'What? You'll *nail* us in?' cries Jamilah. You exchange horrified glances.

'Sometimes police helicopter fly here. Sometimes police boat come to do inspection. They think maybe this fisherman is people smuggler. You must be very, very hidden, so we use nails. Okay?' says Piggy.

It's the third time he's asked you 'Okay?' and you realise now that it's a question with only one answer. It's really *not* okay, but there is no other way, so you swallow your fear and reply, 'Okay.'

The deck of the boat is made of latticed wood, with small square holes through which you can see the sky, and the faces of Piggy and the fisherman as they bend over to nail you in.

Bang. Bang. Every blow of the hammer makes the boat jump.

You hold Jamilah tight as you lie beside her. 'We'll be okay,' you whisper.

Jamilah bites her lip and nods. She is sweating – from fear, or the fever, or both. You remember the feeling of squeezing her hot, damp, frightened body in a hug on the night you made it home after Aunty Rahama died. You stop and correct yourself: after Aunty Rahama *disappeared*.

The pen in your pocket pokes your thigh. If only you had a computer and knew the password to unlock the file called 'My Story'. There must be more information there. Aunty Rahama wouldn't have disappeared without leaving more for you. It's the last piece of the puzzle, you're sure of it.

The trip from Malaysia to Indonesia would usually take five hours by boat, but the fisherman doesn't go directly there – that would look too suspicious to any helicopters overhead.

Instead, he motors out into the water and then does what fishermen actually do: throws nets and waits.

Sometimes fish bodies land on the deck of the boat and a slimy mix of salt water and fish blood drips onto your face. A couple of times, you hear helicopters whirring overhead.

You try to lie as still as a body in a coffin.

Sometimes a restless rage fills your limbs and you want to scream, *Get me out of here! I can't stand it!* but you know there's no alternative.

The sun climbs to its full height. The sea breeze can't reach you down in the hull, and the stench of fish guts and petrol is overpowering. You help Jamilah to sip from the plastic bottle of warm water you have in your hidey-hole. Then you close your eyes and whisper prayers to Allah.

The heat fades out of the day, the engine roars to life again, and the waves bounce beneath your back as the boat skips towards the Indonesian coast. You left before dawn, and now it is getting dark – you've spent around fourteen hours on the water, you guess.

When the nails are removed and you try to stand up, you are so dizzy and stiff that your legs threaten to give way under you.

The Indonesian people smuggler has come to meet you. He yanks you and Jamilah roughly into the thick jungle and leaves you sitting under a tree with broad, yellow-ish leaves a short way from the boat as he goes back and pays the fisherman, then offers him a smoke.

Their cigarette tips glow red as the ruby on the end of your pen. The smell of clove tobacco snakes its way through the jungle in the gathering dark.

You sit under the tree, your limbs shaking, your belly growling. Jamilah slumps beside you and moans quietly. Suddenly, you hear the sound of sirens, wailing like ghosts in the yellow-grey jungle.

The fisherman shouts what can only be a swear word in his language, and he hastily shoves the boat back into the sea, while the other guy runs in the opposite direction. They're leaving you behind.

You yank Jamilah to her feet. You are smuggled goods – children in a country where no one can help you and you don't speak the language. If the police catch you, you're dead meat.

Your feet pound across the leaf-littered jungle floor, away from the sound of the sirens and the smell of the cigarettes. Your breath comes in and out in hot shoves. Jamilah is choking down her coughs, and you are pulling her forward, over buttress roots and ditches, deep into the jungle, where the vines are thickest.

Dropping to your knees, you burrow under a bush and pull Jamilah in too, finding a small space to hide at the heart of the bush, pulling the branches and vines back over you like a curtain.

Leaves crackle beneath you. Distant voices shout. It is almost totally dark inside the bush, and it smells of boggy earth, spicy leaves and stinky squashed insects. Things prickle and tickle your skin. You wait and listen, alert as a rabbit.

Darkness falls on the jungle, and you begin to wonder how much longer you should stay hidden when you see a beam of light rake the ground between the trees.

'Hey,' calls a heavily accented voice in English, 'where are you? Come out, kids. The police are gone. I'll take you to Australia.'

Jamilah's wide, scared eyes reflect a little of the torchlight's shine. She has both hands plastered over her mouth to muffle her coughs. Her body is shaking like a car on a rough road. Her eyes ask an unspoken question: *Is it safe to go out?*

If it's the people smuggler and you stay hidden, he might leave without you. But if it's the police and you reveal yourselves, you'll be thrown into jail. Your ears and eyes are pricked for clues, but it's too dark to see if the man is wearing a uniform, and the accented voice could belong to either.

What should you do?

✦ To stay hidden, go to page 226.

✦ To climb out of the bush, go to page 220.

'I believe you,' you whisper to Jamilah.

You pick up your shoe from the ground by the door, and take out the money.

'We want to go to Italy where our aunty is,' you tell Piggy. 'But you have to use this money to buy medicine for my sister as well, and a Malaysian simcard.'

Piggy takes the money and leaves the room, muttering grumpily, probably disgruntled to be woken at three a.m. to be told to change the plans and buy this and that.

Jamilah's shoulders heave with more coughs. You sit back on the bed and wrap your arms around her, then you drift off into an edgy, fractured sleep. Piggy comes back at ten that morning. He throws a tattered box in your direction.

'Medicine,' he says. 'Tomorrow you will go to Turkey, then Greece. You take boat, Greece to Italy.'

He throws another bag at you.

'Food. No money for simcard.'

The box of medicine has been well used. 'Panadol' is written on the front. Two white tablets remain in the packet; the rest have been popped out of their foil and are gone. It's not enough, but there's nothing you can do about it.

DURING THE FLIGHT to Turkey, every muscle in your body feels like it's at snapping point. You chew on the inside of your cheek; pick at a sliver of loose skin next to your thumbnail; shift from side to side as if someone's made you sit on hot rocks.

You can't shake the tight, wound-up, jumpy hope in your belly that you'll somehow, against all the odds, be reunited with Rahama again. And, oh, what a story you'll have to tell her when you get there. The thought makes you smile, just a little.

The airport in Turkey is noisy and busy. You can smell food and petrol. You cast your eyes around the crowd. Piggy said someone would meet you here, but nobody stands out in the sea of dark hair and hijabs.

Warily, you go outside. You are greeted by a blast of heat and sunshine – Jamilah weakly folds her body into yours. You wait for hours, watching taxis come and go, until you notice a guard with his eye on you.

'Come on, it's not safe to wait any longer,' you tell Jamilah. 'Let's go.'

Most of the traffic seems to be heading in one direction, so you follow it, walking along the side of the road. The street signs use the same alphabet as English, but the words don't make any sense to you. You have no money, and no idea what to do next.

Just then, a fancy black car screeches to a halt next to you. The driver, a man, nods at you as if to say: *Get in*. Thinking this must be the person who was meant to meet you at the airport, you and Jamilah climb into the car.

IT'S BEEN NEARLY three years now, since you took that ride. You've asked yourself so many times, *Could things have worked out differently, if we hadn't got in? Or would he have kidnapped us anyway?*

You knew within minutes of getting in the car, that it wasn't his intention to take you safely to Italy. You still have nightmares about it. The man smuggled you out of Turkey, drugged and bound, and passed you along a chain of criminal hands: people who make their profit by kidnapping vulnerable children. Jamilah was passed in a different direction. She could be anywhere.

You weren't even sure which country you'd ended up in at first – just that it was bitingly cold, with pale-faced people who spoke in guttural voices; a place where the colour seemed to have leached out of the sky. Now, you're pretty sure it's Russia, or one of its neighbouring countries.

You work in a match factory. You aren't paid. The owners say you owe the people smuggler thousands of dollars for your journey and have to work here until you've repaid him.

You've been beaten more times than you can remember. Sometimes, your fingertips are so cold when you work the machine that you're not even sure you'd notice if one of them were sliced right off.

But you suppose you would still feel the pain. You're a human: you breathe, you bleed, you struggle. Even when you don't want to anymore. Even when Allah seems to have deserted you, and the hot, spicy-smelling streets of Mogadishu seem like a lifetime ago.

You work, and you survive, and you keep a tiny flame of hope alive that, one day, you will find a way to escape.

THE END

✦ To return to your last choice and try again, go to page 202

You clamber out of the bush, pins-and-needles shooting down your legs. The torchlight instantly swings towards you.

'Hello,' calls the same heavily accented voice. 'How many of you are there?'

'Just two,' you say, pulling Jamilah out of the bush, and then – too late! – you realise your mistake. If this was the people smuggler, he would already know there are only two of you. It must be the police!

Still holding tight to Jamilah's arm, you start to run. Vines lash at your bare arms, and the trees seem to bounce wildly in the torchlight as the man behind you blows a whistle and runs after you. The ground is a tangle of roots and holes, and Jamilah is trying her best to keep up but keeps falling heavily against your arm every few steps.

The policeman's footsteps are closing in, and you can hear that more of his colleagues have joined in the chase, shouting to each other in Indonesian as they run.

You glance over your shoulder to see how far

behind you the policeman is, and he closes the remaining gap in only a few bounds, his eyes and teeth shining in the torchlight, his breath loud and menacing.

He grabs Jamilah, and she squeals and wriggles violently. You throw your full body weight at him, aiming to headbutt him in the nose, but he dodges nimbly and you miss, only clipping the side of his body and lurching face-first into the leaf litter.

The other policemen are on you now, and they use their batons to beat you on your thighs, shoulders, back and arms. You throw your arms over your head to protect it from the beating, and then you feel a tight, cold band of metal snap shut around your wrists. One of the officers hauls you to your feet by the handcuffs he's just placed on you.

In the Indonesian jail, you are separated from Jamilah, and this hurts much more than the bruises from where the batons hit you, or your stomach, which aches from hunger after your long day on the boat. You are in an adult cell: a concrete room with filthy bunks and iron bars, which you share with about forty men.

The roughest of the prisoners pick fights with the other men, steal their food, and bribe cigarettes from the jailors. They have skin laced with homemade tattoos, and their teeth are broken and brown. This prison is their den. They are known here, and feared. You try to stay as invisible as possible.

You have only one hope to get you and Jamilah out of here: to offer the cash Abshir gave you to a jailer as a bribe. The bag you had with some food, drink, and the phone was taken when you were arrested. But the pen in your pocket and the money in your shoe luckily went untouched. For forty-eight hours, you watch the jailers come and go, sensing who's brutal, who's a soft touch, who can be corrupted.

You pick a young jailer who you have seen reading an English-language magazine. His hair is slicked to one side, his eyes are hopeful, and his tan uniform is clean. You almost think he might be too 'good' to accept a bribe – but then you see him lingering dreamily on the magazine page that advertises a car. He's poor. He wants better things.

You wait until he comes close to the bars and then, catching his eye, you lean forward and whisper your offer to him.

He's tempted. You can almost see, in his faraway gaze, a reflection of a tiny car, his hand on the wheel, his arm round a girl, a sunset over the ocean as the engine purrs. But then he turns away and pretends he hasn't heard you. Your heart sinks.

Later that day, a different jailer takes you out of your cell for a 'check-up'. The other prisoners watch you suspiciously. You're frightened that you're about to be punished for having dared to offer a bribe.

But the jailer takes you to a tiny office room, and Jamilah is there, sitting on a plastic chair. She bursts into tears at the sight of you. Her skin and hair are filthy. Her stick-thin shoulders shake as she gives an awful hacking cough, flecks of blood staining her hand and lips. You help her to stand; you can see she's almost too weak to walk.

The officer who brought you to the room slams the door and strides away. You stand in the middle of the room, holding Jamilah, not knowing what to do next.

The door opens again, and the same officer you offered the bribe to walks in. The first thing he does is check the door is locked behind him.

'All right, where's the money?' he asks.

You slip off your shoe and take out three hundred dollars, leaving you a hundred and fifty still hidden under the sole. But the jailer shakes his head.

'Not enough,' he says.

So you add the final hundred and fifty. 'That's all I have,' you insist. 'Really.'

'Not enough,' insists the young jailer again. 'Five hundred is minimum.'

Since Piggy took fifty dollars of your money to get Jamilah a crappy box of used headache tablets, you're fifty short of fulfilling the bribe. There's only one last thing you have to offer: the pen.

You look at Jamilah and know that it would spell her death to send her back inside the jail, even for a few more days. You take the pen from your pocket.

'It's real gold,' you tell him. 'Worth more than fifty dollars.'

After that, the jailer moves so quickly and smoothly to get you out of jail that it's clear he's done this before.

You and Jamilah are ejected onto the streets of Jakarta, Indonesia. You are homeless, penniless, starving, and Jamilah is horribly sick. Your pen is gone, you have no access to a phone, and anyone who knows you and might help is thousands of kilometres away. You don't speak the language, and any police officer who finds you here without papers could throw you back into jail, from where, next time, there would be no escape.

Looking around, you can see at a glance that there are lots of other people like you in Jakarta, living on a thread of hope day to day, getting by on their wits alone.

It's the same in every city in the world, you realise now. Maybe it's even like this in Australia. If you take the shiny lid off, turn a city upside down and shake it, all the poor people will tumble out like pebbles.

You look down at Jamilah. *At least we're two pebbles together*, you think. You hope you'll be able to survive.

THE END

✷ To return to your last choice and try again, go to page 215.

You breathe as slowly and quietly as you can and shake your head at Jamilah. You're not moving until you can be sure it's safe to come out – no matter how long it takes.

'Come on, kids,' says the voice. 'I'm not going to hurt you.'

You've heard enough Somali folktales by now, like the one about the persuasive cat and the innocent mouse, to know that the only people who call out 'I'm not going to hurt you' are usually the ones who want to.

Eventually, the torch swings around and the footsteps crunch away.

You stay in the bush all night. Mosquitoes whine and bite your arms and legs. Jamilah coughs so much she gags. You wipe the sweaty hair and gritty bits of bark and dirt from her forehead.

Just before dawn, when monkeys are hooting and crashing through the branches above, and cracks of pink light are slipping through the leaves, you hear another person approach. They are stomping, and muttering what can only be Indonesian curses. Then they give a shout in English.

'Okay, kids! If you hear me, then come out, you bloody...' He lapses into Indonesian swearing again. Then he shouts, in a voice wilder than the monkeys: 'Big punch on my face! Can't see from one eye! My car taken, and I spend the night in jail, and now I pay bloody big fine! All to come back and look for you! If you're still here, you did very good, but come out *now* or I bloody leave and not come back!'

The voice is so indignant, and the stomping so heated, you're sure it's your man. The police couldn't be that good at acting. You can see glimpses of his clothes now, and he's not in uniform, although in the dim pre-dawn light you can't get a clear look at his face.

Then you smell clove cigarettes.

'That's him,' you say to Jamilah. You climb out of the bush and call, 'Hey! We're over here!'

The people smuggler, who has a horrible puffed-up purple eyelid from his encounter with the police, is relieved to see you, and he actually congratulates you for hiding so well. He doesn't get his share of the money until you reach Australia, so lost refugees mean lost income for him.

As he helps you into his car, he tells you his name is Budi. It's a long drive to Cisarua, the village south of Jakarta where you'll be staying. For three days you eat and sleep in the car, until you finally reach a large white house on the side of a hill on a ramshackle, leafy street in Cisarua. Budi doesn't lock you in a basement room like Piggy did – you are free to come and go as you wish, but he warns you against drawing attention to yourself on the streets.

The house is full of about twenty other asylum seekers, who so far all seem to be men. Mattresses line the hallways. Everybody shares the one kitchen and toilet. When you and Jamilah go to the kitchen for some water, some pale men with thick eyebrows and dark hair sitting at the kitchen table eye you morosely. You say hello in English, but they simply shrug then go back to their card game. You wonder where they've come from.

You and Jamilah return to the bedroom Budi allocated to you and sit uneasily on the one thin mattress that's on the floor. About six more mattresses have been pulled to one side and stacked against the wall. You take out your pen and twirl it between your fingertips.

Just then, there's a knock at the door. You whip the pen away just before the door opens a fraction and a woman appears. She has similar features to the men who were sitting around the table, wears a navy-blue hijab, and rests one hand on her pregnant belly. In the other hand she holds a bowl of noodles with two forks. She doesn't speak, just holds the bowl out and smiles.

'Thank you!' cries Jamilah, and the woman nods happily as Jamilah takes the bowl.

'What's your name? And what country do you come from?' you ask her.

She thinks for a second, working through the English. Then she whispers softly: 'I am Maryam. My husband, Majid. We from Iran. We stay...Indonesia...two years now.'

She looks at her belly sadly. Then one of the men from the kitchen calls something in her language, and she turns to go.

'Wait!' you cry. 'Did you say two *years*?'

'Yes,' Maryam replies, turning back to you. 'Two years, three months. We...no more money to pay smuggler. First try no good.' Her voice is resigned, but gentle.

You share some of the noodles with Jamilah. She's too tired to finish eating, and her forehead still feels hot to touch. So you go out, with a few of the American dollars from your stash in your pocket, to see if you can buy more food, medicine, and a local simcard.

Abshir will be relieved to hear that you made it this far, and maybe it's time to call Aadan too, and tell him you'll be seeing him soon.

You walk down the steep street, looking at some pigs snuffling through rubbish piles, happy children running off to school, trees with unripe bananas beginning to fruit.

You wonder how long you could survive, treading water, in a place like this before you ran out of money or met with some bad luck. Budi's bruised eye has hinted at a violent and corrupt world lying beneath this seemingly pleasant scene.

There's a money-changing machine just at the bottom of the street, and a place that sells you an Indonesian simcard. It's a relief to hear Abshir's voice at last.

'Walaal!' he shouts. 'Man, you'd better call your Uncle Aadan right now, before he flies over here and personally chops my head off!'

'Why, what's wrong?'

'I couldn't keep it from him – he called for you, and I told him what's happened. But he doesn't get it! He says I shouldn't have sent you alone – it's too dangerous, you know, all of that. I said, "Walaal, these kids are fighters, they'll make it!" And let's face it, you'd be dead by now if you'd stayed. There just wasn't another way. I tried to tell him! But he might forgive me, at least a little bit, if you call him straight away. He's worried sick!'

You call Aadan, and he shouts in relief, then immediately starts firing advice and warnings at you like a bossy grandma. You have to interrupt him so you can tell him about Rahama.

'Jamilah's certain she saw her,' you tell him. 'In Italy, being pulled out of the sea. Jamilah had a fever and I didn't believe her at first, but then *I* saw Zayd, in the very same clip.'

There is a stunned silence at the end of the phone.

You go on: 'I *know* she wouldn't leave us without letting us know. If Jamilah's right – if she's alive – there has to be more about this on the password-protected "My Story" file on the pen. But I couldn't guess the password. Can you think of anything?'

There's more stunned silence. Just as you're about to ask if he's still there, Aadan's voice croaks: '*Freedom*. The ruby in the pen, it's one of the seven Freedom Gems. That might be the password.'

In your hurry to end the call and try this as the password, you almost forget to thank him. It's only after you've hung up that you wonder what he meant by *one of the seven Freedom Gems*. It's yet another question for you to find an answer to when you reach Australia.

You pay to use a computer and unscrew the pen. Thank goodness the desert sand, bilge water in the boat hull, and everything else it's been through haven't damaged the little memory stick at all – it hums and opens.

Your breath quickens as you click on 'My Story'.

'This file is password protected. Please enter your password.'

The last time you saw these words was with Sampson, just before you hacked al-Shabaab's bank account. So many things have happened since then. Your hands shake as you type in the seven letters: f...r...e...e...d...o...m...

There's a moment's pause as the computer thinks, then...it opens like a flower.

My darlings,

This is the hardest letter I've ever written.
I have started it in fifty different ways, and deleted them all. But it all comes down to this...

Al-Shabaab are coming for me. They know about the interview with Zayd, and the investigation into Bright Dream. This afternoon, they plan to detonate a bomb at the broadcasting building.

I want al-Shabaab to believe that this bomb kills me. I want the world to think I'm dead – yes, even you, my darlings. I'm going to try to save all our lives, by pretending to lose my own.

I know their plans, because Zayd wasn't killed by al-Shabaab: he escaped from them when the car they were in crashed. Worrying that he'd put our lives at risk by telling us about Bright Dream, he contacted someone who owed him a favour who was still inside al-Shabaab. He confirmed that a spy in the broadcasting company had warned them about me.

It's over for me here now. For so long as al-Shabaab believes I'm alive, they'll come after me. And if they find out about you two children they will use you as bait – kidnap you, torture you, threaten to kill you – because they would see you are my weak point. The only way I can protect you is by making them think I am gone, once and for all, so they will give up.

So, I've made a plan. I will go to work at the scheduled time for the broadcast this afternoon. I will place my red hijab by a window, where everyone can see it to believe I'm in the building, so al-Shabaab will feel sure they've killed me. None of my colleagues will be there; I've sent them all a fake invitation to a meeting across town.

I will sneak out the back door, and make my way to the Ethiopian border, where Zayd will be waiting for me. Whatever it takes, we'll find our way to safety. Aadan and I have promised each other that we'll make a home together with you two kids, a wonderful new home in Australia. It's a promise I plan to keep.

I know it will probably take you a while after I give you the pen to find my note, contact Aadan, work out the password and open this file. I know that keeping the full story from you for this long is going to cause you pain, and I'm sorry. It's the only way I can ensure I have time to get well out of Somalia without you trying to follow me, risking al-Shabaab learning of and following you.

It's okay if you're angry, confused or upset with me when you read this. One day, we'll be together again, and I can answer your questions, and maybe you'll forgive me for leaving you this way. I don't know how far away that day will be – I only pray that it comes soon. I love you more than words can say.

Now, I must go and find you, and give you this pen. The biggest journey of my life begins then. Whatever comes next is Allah's will.

Never stop fighting for freedom.

I love you so much.
Aunty Rahama

You sit, staring at the computer. You want to whoop with joy that Rahama didn't die in the bomb blast, but you are paralysed with confusion. You read the letter for a second, and then a third time, struggling to make sense of the storm of questions whirling in your brain.

So Jamilah was right, she did see Aunty Rahama being rescued in Italy … but why are she and Zayd there, and not in Australia? And why has no one heard from them since?

Your thoughts are interrupted by a commotion taking place outside. Rising from the computer, you go to the door and see Maryam coming down the hill, struggling to run, holding her belly, looking around wildly. People are staring. She sees you and shouts, and the panic in her voice makes your insides freeze for one terrible moment. Then you run to her.

'Your sister!' she pants when you reach her. 'She, she …' Maryam is gasping for breath and can't find the right English word. 'Not dead. But not wake up! Please come *now*!'

You sprint up the hill, leaving the woman behind, your limbs on fire. *Jamilah!*

You gasp a prayer in time with your pumping limbs: *Don't die, don't die, don't die.*

When you reach her, Jamilah is conscious again. One of the Iranian men is helping her to sit up on the bed and sip some water. Her face is dangerously ashen and there are red flecks around her lips where she has been coughing more blood. She looks at you and manages a trembly smile.

'She's very sick,' says the Iranian man, who you guess is Maryam's husband, Majid. 'Like my nephew, who had tuberculosis. Does she have it?'

At that moment, Maryam enters, breathing hard. Majid rises quickly to shepherd her out of the room.

'My wife shouldn't be near you – it is too dangerous,' he calls back over his shoulder. 'But I will return to help.'

Is it tuberculosis? you wonder, gripped with anxiety. *People can die of that.*

You kneel in front of Jamilah, a lump in your throat.

'You have to survive this, chickpea,' you tell her, using Aunty Rahama's old nickname for her. 'Because you were right – you *did* see Aunty Rahama. I just read a letter she wrote on the day the bomb went off, and she knew it was coming! She made it, she's *alive*...so you've got to make it too, okay?' Hot tears begin to spill down your cheeks.

Jamilah gazes at you in astonishment and delight. Then she begins to sob too. You hold her, and you cry together – not from happiness alone, or just plain sadness; you cry with a broken heart that's filled with sun.

Jamilah lifts her hot, wet face away from your neck, and manages to say: 'Budi came. The boat's going *tonight*.'

It's only then that you register the buzz of activity you ran through when you came back into the house – people stuffing food and their meagre belongings into bags, clasping photos of their loved ones, fear and hope on their faces…

The only people who weren't focussed on preparing to go were Maryam and Majid, who've been here two years already. You guess that they won't be going anywhere.

'I don't think we should go tonight,' you say to Jamilah. 'You're too sick for a risky boat journey. We could rest here, and go next time.'

'No!' cries Jamilah. 'Budi said he doesn't know when there'll be another boat.'

Jamilah breaks off to cough. She struggles to catch her breath, and you feel your stomach churn with apprehension.

'We have to go tonight!' she bursts out. 'There might not be the right medicine for me here, anyway. If our money runs out, we'll be stuck here like Maryam and Majid.'

Your stomach clenches into a fist as you imagine a black, restless ocean and your sister burning with fever, struggling to breathe as the boat is tossed about. It's the most dangerous thing you could do right now – but it's also the fastest route to safety. Will you take it?

<hr />

✳ If you stay in Indonesia to give Jamilah time to rest, go to page 239.

✳ If you make the boat journey tonight, go to page 243.

You shake your head firmly. 'We have enough money to survive here for a while, and Aadan will send us more if we need him to.'

Jamilah opens her mouth to protest. 'Stop,' you tell her. 'Save your breath for getting better.'

You find Maryam and Majid in the kitchen. 'Do you think it's possible to buy the medicine we need here?' you ask.

'Yes, I think so,' says Majid. 'In Iran, I was a pharmacist. We will help you.'

'Oh, thank you,' you say to the kind-hearted couple. 'Then we're staying here too.'

Majid goes out to buy antibiotics that can help with diseases like tuberculosis, and you feel an immense sense of relief to have somebody who knows what he's doing help you with this.

THE WEEKS PASS. Jamilah's antibiotics slowly take effect, and by the third week she is walking about a little and eating more. You are both overjoyed, but Majid warns that tuberculosis can easily reoccur if a patient is not healthy and strong enough to fight off another attack.

You bide your time, and the weeks turn into months. You continue to stay in the big white house on the hill, where a train of other asylum seekers come and go but you, Jamilah, Majid and Maryam stay on, the everlasting veterans. You spend most of your days playing cards and practising English.

Occasionally you go to the shops to receive money transfers from Aadan, and you call him regularly. You always pray that he'll have found some clues to Aunty Rahama's whereabouts, but he never has.

'I have to warn you about something,' he says uneasily one day.

'What?' you ask, worried he's heard some bad news about Aunty Rahama.

'Oh, it's nothing too bad, but…there are lots of arguments about boat people in the Australian news at the moment.'

'What the heck are boat people?' you ask, imagining people who look like boats, or who live on boats.

Aadan laughs. 'People like *you* – who come to Australia by boat, or who want to. There's a big stink in the media about it. *Stop the boats, stop the boats, stop the bloody boats.*'

'Would they mind if we arrived by helicopter?' you joke.

'That's the thing, they probably wouldn't,' he replies. 'Most asylum seekers here come by plane on a student or tourist visa. I just wanted to warn you the government's trying to look tough at the moment. Soon you might *never* be able to settle here if you come by boat. And you know people drown on that trip. Boats sink all the time.' He heaves a huge sigh. 'I still can't find Rahama. I can't lose you too. Please, stay there and wait for the UNHCR. As kids alone, you'll have a better chance at a visa than most.'

When you tell Majid about your conversation with Aadan, he rolls his eyes. 'The UNHCR does nothing here,' he tells you heavily. 'It's impossible to get a visa with them. One tiny office, a couple of staff, and thousands of people on the waiting list to even apply in the first place.'

'We're on the waiting list too,' you tell him. Aadan advised you and Jamilah to visit Jakarta to register with the UNHCR and put your name down for an appointment, which you did – months ago.

'Don't hold your breath,' jokes Majid darkly. 'Most people I know waited nearly a year to get their first appointment – I'm not exaggerating.'

He sighs deeply and looks around the room to make sure Maryam's in a different part of the house.

'I hate myself for bringing her here,' he confesses in a whisper. 'The Iranian government jailed me and tortured me for participating in pro-democracy protests. When they let me out, I was so starved and beaten up, my own mother hardly recognised me. If I ever go back, I'll be killed. Now my child will be born here, with no opportunity to go to school or get a job. I've told Maryam to just divorce me and go home, but she won't.'

Majid grips your hand, and his dark eyes have a burning intensity.

'You kids have the best years of your life ahead of you. Don't waste them here,' he urges. 'If you can get to Australia, just go. Tell Budi you'll get on the next boat – I would. Jamilah's well enough now.'

You don't know what to think. Aadan has warned you that the situation in Australia is getting more hostile – but Majid seems to think there's not much hope here, either. Once again, you face a choice between bad and worse – but which option is worse?

<hr />

✳ To wait for the UNHCR and hope for a visa, go to page 271.

✳ To go by boat to Australia as soon as possible, go to page 287.

✳ To read a fact file on life in limbo, turn to page 319, then return to this page to make your choice.

You look into Jamilah's eyes. 'Are you sure you want to go tonight? This boat trip will be even rougher and longer than the last one.' She nods resolutely.

'Okay then, let's do it,' you say, although fear grips your stomach.

As darkness falls over the white house on the hill that night, two mini-vans pull up outside, mosquitoes swarming to their headlights.

You and Jamilah crowd into one of the vans along with about fifteen other people from the house. The only things you have on you are a bottle of water, which Majid and Maryam pushed into your hands as you left, the pen, the money inside your shoe, and your phone. Budi instructed you all not to bring anything more.

The road to the coast is littered with potholes, and the driver looks grim as he swerves to avoid them. You think that his ears, like yours, must be pricked for the sound of sirens coming to bust you.

You arrive at the coast and the van parks. You can hear the sound of waves crashing. The dread in your stomach rises, until it seems to be sloshing back and forth like the waves. This is it. Your only chance.

The mini-van doors roar as the driver drags them open. You climb out in the company of the crowd. Four other mini-vans are already parked in the moonlight, each disgorging a crowd of about twenty stooped passengers, who clutch each other and look about like rabbits.

You hear the scrunching of footsteps on sand and the thump and hiss of waves. The drivers of the vans, and a few more Indonesian men who were waiting here for you, mutter orders as they herd you down to the beach. You squeeze Jamilah's hand. It is slick with sweat.

People crane their necks, trying to see over each other's heads to get a look at the boat. You and Jamilah wriggle through to the front.

There is a small boat flailing in the shallows – like the ones that used to go out at Lido Beach, with a crew of around twelve fishermen. In silhouette, you see a long, narrow deck, and a boxy wheelhouse where the driver stands. *That must be the boat they'll use to take us out, a dozen at a time, to a larger one*, you think. *We'll have to wade out to this one first: I hope it's not too deep.*

It won't be your first time in the ocean, but because the fighting in Mogadishu has been so bad in recent years, it hasn't been safe enough to spend a lot of time at the beach. Neither you or Jamilah are confident swimmers.

The people smugglers don't give you time to ask questions or react – they just begin herding people into the water, roughly, barking: 'Go! Go!'

Two wiry Indonesian fishermen on the boat start reaching overboard and hauling people up onto the deck – their new heavy, sodden catch.

As people around you stagger in, children are crying and parents are hoisting them up higher to keep them dry. You can see the question in their eyes: *Are you sure we can do this?* and the reply: *We* are *doing this. Come.*

You're standing at the edge of the water, feeling it splash over your feet, when one of the drivers pushes you in the back, and you stumble forward, into water up to your knees, Jamilah's arm wrapped tightly around your waist. A wave reaches up and slaps you in the stomach, and she squeals because she's only short and it's closer to her face.

You reach the splintery side of the boat and a pair of strong brown hands lift Jamilah, then you, out of the water. You see a trapdoor in the deck leading to storage space below, but you don't want to climb in there, so you shuffle to the edge of the deck on the other side of the boat, where at least you can hold on to a rail.

The crowd shifts and tightens as more and more people are crammed on board. No one is shoving, though, because everyone is thinking: *We only have to stay on this boat for a little while, until we get to the larger one.*

THERE IS NO larger boat. You only realise this once the journey is so far underway that there's no way you can rebel – when the black waves are heaving under the thin hull, the distant lights of the shore have faded, and the sound of seasick passengers retching and children sobbing fill the night air.

You are going to Australia on *this*: the boat of two impoverished fishermen who have been talked into a lucrative and dangerous job; a boat that looks as if it's never left Indonesian waters; a boat made to hold a dozen fishermen and their nets.

Some people are crammed into the hull, a space below deck that's at least free from the saltwater spray. When you and Jamilah peek inside, you see that the parents have taken their young children down here, seeking shelter.

'When will we be in Australia?' ask the children

in their languages. You don't speak Farsi, Tamil or Hazaragi, but you know what they're asking.

Their parents stroke their brows and reply, 'Soon, my darling, soon.'

You don't try to squeeze into the hull – you'd rather you and Jamilah have the air and a little more space. You position yourself near the front of the boat, where you can see the waves coming and anticipate the rise and crashing drop of the boat.

The engine revs, working hard, giving the occasional cough. Jamilah's body leans up against yours; she is conscious, but so weak and feverish now that you hold her tightly to stop her slipping into the ocean.

'I wonder if Aunty Rahama was scared when she crossed the ocean too,' she whispers to you.

'She probably was,' you acknowledge. 'But being brave doesn't mean you never get scared. Brave is when you know you're afraid but you do it anyway.' You draw Jamilah close. 'She'll be so proud of us when we finally see her again,' you say.

Jamilah falls asleep, but you stay awake so you can keep holding her safely, the thought of Rahama burning in your mind like a candle of hope through the night.

DAWN ARRIVES, AND the waves die down. The sea looks almost beautiful, pink and golden, but you know it's still as hostile as a desert. The boat's little engine chugs on.

The passengers begin to organise themselves. The people smugglers have packed cakes of dry noodles and plastic drums full of water to last you the journey, and the boat has a small camping stove that the fishermen usually cook their dinner on. An agreement is reached that one of the men, a muscly young guy from Afghanistan called Ali, will cook all of today's noodles in one big batch and share them out.

Ali crams the noodles into a large pot, reaches for the plastic water drum and sloshes a large amount of water over the noodles.

A sharp, toxic smell fills the air. Some other passengers shout, 'Whoa whoa whoa!' and jump to stop him. But it's too late – Ali has just tipped petrol, not water, all over the noodles.

A wild shouting-match starts up. Ali waves his arm at the drums, defending himself, and you can see that the water drums and petrol drums *do* look just the same.

An older Afghani man slaps Ali's face, and his wife grabs his arm to calm him down, but many of the other passengers just stare out to sea, eyes narrowed against the glare of the sun and water.

The problem is now not only hunger, because you have petrol in your noodles, but also fuel, because you have noodles in your petrol.

Some of the passengers begin diligently draining as much of the petrol back into the drum as they can, carefully using a rag to filter out the swimming noodle strands. The fishermen mutter angrily and exchange worried calculations, clearly considering whether you'll still have enough petrol for the journey. But if they do reach a conclusion, they don't share it with you.

The sun is relentless. People take turns drinking from the black plastic cap from the water drum, careful not to spill a drop. The fishermen produce a single blue tarpaulin and string it up between the wheel-house roof and one of the sides, to act as a shade-cloth. People take turns to cram under the shade-cloth and into the stifling but shaded hole below deck. Children and the elderly are given special consideration.

The day slowly passes, the gnawing hole of hunger in your stomach dulling off to a background moan, as you've found hunger does if you ignore it long enough. The waves slap the hull and the engine putters on.

Night falls, and you endure another long night by dreaming of life in Australia. Another scorching day, another night, and then a third day go by, yet there's still no sign of land.

There was enough water in the large plastic drums on board for all the passengers to share sips for three days, but now the last drum is getting low and light. You wonder if this means not enough water was packed, or that you have become lost.

People have fallen, for the most part, into an anxious, haggard silence. There is nothing left to do but wait, and pray.

Darkness falls once again, the wind picks up, and you manage to sleep for a while under the tarp with Jamilah.

When you wake up, the boat is … you search your mind for the English word you heard on the plane to Malaysia … *experiencing turbulence*. The waves are so steep that your bum rises right off the deck and seems to hang in mid-air before plummeting downwards again.

Jamilah is so weak that you have to hold her as the boat smacks the surface, to cushion her from flopping forwards and smacking her face on the deck. People are starting to moan; many are vomiting again. Spray hits your face. The fishermen are looking tense, both gripping the steering wheel.

People start pouring out from below deck – water has started forcing its way through the cracks in the hull. A human chain is formed to bail the water out with a bucket. The wind rises to a howl. The human chain can hardly keep up, using only their single bucket.

You hear a groaning, wrenching sound, which can only be the boat's timbers starting to tear apart and nails squealing away from wood in pointed rows. You clamber to your feet. The deck's surface is slick with brine. Nausea builds in your throat from terror and seasickness.

You are holding Jamilah up, both of you trying to stand upright as the boat bucks your bodies around. You are so drenched by the waves that it takes you a while to notice that the deck is now ankle-deep in water. The boat is going down.

The fishermen have given up trying to steer and are now shouting at their passengers in Indonesian, but no one can understand them. Then they use their radio to send an SOS distress call. Some people are praying loudly – you recognise the word 'Allah', shouted to the stars. You pray that you're close enough to Australia that someone might rescue you. Your eyes scan the horizon, and you think you make out a lumpy dark mass that stays still among the lurching waves. Rocks? An island?

Huge bubbles rise out from under the deck as the hull fills with water. People scream as the deck sinks deeper and the water starts creeping up your legs. Some people are scrambling onto the wheel-house roof, which causes the whole boat to tilt, plunging people off the sides into the inky water, which churns with thrashing people scrambling to climb back aboard. The sound of children's sobs rises above the scene like a terrible song.

Your body is pounding with anticipation – your stomach clenched tight, your hands tingling with adrenaline – but you find that your mind is filled with a floodlit beam of focus.

I'm going to save us.

The water is up to your knees now. From the corner of your eye, you see that one of the big near-empty plastic water drums has started to float away from the boat.

'Jump!' you shout to Jamilah, and with all your strength you launch off the side of the boat, away from the splashing crowds and the debris, towards the plastic drum, Jamilah at your side.

The saltwater forces its way up your nose with a burning intensity. You keep a fistful of Jamilah's clothes in one hand, and thrash frantically towards the drum bobbing just out of reach, your head slipping up and down between air and sea.

You reach the drum, struggling to hold it still as you haul Jamilah up onto it. She hugs the drum with her arms and rests her head against it, while you grip it by a handle from below, up to your neck in the water, panting hard.

The water is cold, and your soaked clothes cling and balloon heavily. The night air is filled with screams and sobs.

You see a mother in the water near you, her head nearly underwater as she struggles to lift her baby higher than herself. You keep a tight hold on the drum and kick desperately towards them, reaching them just as the waves close over the woman's hijab. You haul her up, and she lies sobbing with her face against the plastic drum, holding her wailing baby close.

You bob in the inky, deep blackness, gasping and looking around wildly. A few men are swimming away from the wreck, heading for the black shape you thought you saw earlier – it is a rocky outcrop in the ocean! If there are rocks jutting out of the water, then surely you're not too far from the coastline of Australia?

If you could make it to the rocks, pulling Jamilah and the mother and baby along, you'd all be able to climb up out of the water. You might then be able to take the plastic drum back to the wreck to rescue others. But the rocks are a long way away.

Just then, one of the fishermen fires a flare, which rockets into the sky above the boat in a blazing trail of orange smoke. It hovers overhead like a hissing star.

Is there anyone out there to see it? you wonder. *Did anyone hear our distress call?*

What if you set out for the rocks and a boat comes to the wreck to save everyone? You might not be found. But if nobody comes, then up on the rocks is the best place to be…

You look back at the rocks and see a tiny black figure – one of the swimmers has reached the rocks. He jumps up and down, waving his arms. He made it!

Will you try to make it too?

✦ If you swim for the rocks, go to page 267.
✦ If you stay with the boat, go to page 255.

Water slaps your face and you cough, trying to heave yourself a little higher onto the drum. It bucks under you, in danger of tipping off Jamilah and the woman with her baby. The rocks are too far away in seas this rough, you decide – it's best to cling to the drum and stay with the wreck.

The flare still casts an eerie red light over the scene. The rim of the deck is still just above the waterline, and you see the fishermen' silhouettes hunched over their radio, broadcasting a call for help for as long as they can. The water around them churns with people, many trying to clamber up onto the wreckage, their weight only sending it down faster.

Jamilah's wide eyes are shining in the dim moonlight as she takes in the scene around you. Even through this chaos, you can hear a faint rasping noise as she struggles to force each breath in and out. You pray that she doesn't faint again.

You touch her hand and her eyes snap onto yours. 'We'll be okay,' you whisper. 'We'll be okay.'

She nods. Inside, you hate yourself for choosing

this night, this boat, this journey, when you knew she was so sick.

Then your ears pick out a new sound: a bassline that thrums under the wailing of wind and voice, a steady *chug-chug-chug* that seems to be getting louder.

A spotlight drenches the scene, making the boat behind it into a huge black silhouette. Is it a container ship? Another fishing boat?

'*Angkatan laut* Australia *kedatangan!*' whoops one of the fishermen, waving his arms about wildly, and the water erupts into sobs of joy and desperate squeals as the black ship surges towards you.

You keep pedalling your legs through the water. *Hurry, hurry, please hurry.*

A few minutes later, a rubber dinghy buzzes closer, with a woman in uniform at the bow. She takes the baby, then hauls up the mother, then Jamilah.

You grab the edge of the boat with both arms. It's slippery, and heaving up and down with the waves. With a final, awkward move, the navy officer yanks you up by the seat of your pants, and you lurch over the edge of the boat into a sprawling, wet heap.

For a few moments, you just breathe, your cheek still against the rubber floor.

We made it. We made it.

Relief unspools through your veins and you want to sob, but no tears come.

You look up, and see Jamilah being wrapped in a blanket by the concerned navy officer. Instinctively, you touch your pocket, and feel the hard shape of the pen beneath your fingertips. The tears begin to flow then: salt mingling with salt.

YOU DISEMBARK THE navy boat at dawn the next morning. You have been taken to Christmas Island – an Australian island about halfway between the Australian mainland and Indonesia. This was where your ruined fishing boat was aiming for, too.

You were warned back in Indonesia that it's still a long way from the Australian mainland – and that you might be held there for months, even more than a year, while you wait for your visa. But it is Australia. You will be safe.

Now you see that there's a centre on the island surrounded by high-security fences, with guards everywhere. Your stomach curdles – this place looks like a jail.

Inside the centre, though, there are dormitories full of bunk beds, and a canteen for meals. The staff seem friendly – at least in the family section where you are sent. To your great relief, there's also a doctor, who immediately prescribes Jamilah the right antibiotics to treat her tuberculosis.

After you've been there only a few days, you're called in – without Jamilah – for an interview with immigration. An older boy in detention with you, Omar from Sudan, has warned you that this interview could make or break your chances of getting an Australian visa. Omar's already been here a year and a half. Your palms are damp with sweat as you walk into the beige, boxy room.

The woman sitting on the other side of the desk wears a white shirt and has a government ID card on a green cord around her neck.

'I'm Hilary,' she says, shaking your hand. She has a blonde ponytail and a sharp, straight nose.

Hilary fires questions at you, and begins taking notes. Even though you speak English well enough not to need an interpreter, soon your head is swimming as she asks you to recall precise dates and locations of your birth, your parents' death, the flight number on which you left Nairobi…

In parts where your recollections are hazy, she grills you like you're a witness in a courtroom. You can feel your heart beginning to pound, and your confidence wilting.

'Wait!' you say, and you hold up your hand. 'I want to show you...this.'

You bring out Rahama's pen. *Now she'll understand my journey*, you think.

The ruby on its tip glows softly, seeming to murmur to you: *Have courage. We're almost there.*

You begin to explain what this pen is for, and how you came to have it. Hilary's eyebrows knit together. She drums her fingers on the table, looking at you askance.

'Right,' she says eventually, cutting you off. She sounds confused and impatient. 'Look, I'm not sure how you managed to bring this into detention, but technically it's a forbidden item, so...' She reaches out to take it from you.

'*No!*' you shout, rising from your chair and slamming your hand on the table. The force of your shout has taken both you and Hilary by surprise. Part of you feels worried that you might have just damaged your chances for a visa, but you can't stop.

'Do you have *any idea* what I went through for this pen? Where it's been?' you cry. 'I carried it out of Somalia buried under rolls of carpet. I put my friend's life at risk when I opened it on his computer in Kenya. I kept it in Dadaab even when we had nothing else left in the world, and when people tried to kill me for it there, I carried it across the desert and out of Africa, only to take it on two boat journeys that nearly killed my sister and me!'

You pause to draw breath. Hilary looks astonished.

'I don't know if you have someone special in your life,' you continue, in a quieter voice now but one heavy with tears. 'Your parents, a husband, someone you would do anything for... My Aunty Rahama was that person for Jamilah and me. She had to fake her own death to get out of Somalia, thanks to what's on a memory stick inside this pen. We still don't know where she is. But there's information on this pen that could lead to the arrest of some of the most evil terrorists in the world, and help to free hundreds of child soldiers. If there's someone in your life whom you love as much as I love Rahama, you'll understand why I did what I did.'

Hilary nods slowly. She reaches over to the pen. You flinch.

'It's all right, I'm not going to take it from you,' she says.

You sit down again. She unscrews the pen, gives a little gasp when she sees the memory stick there as you described, and plugs it into her computer.

There is a long moment of silence as she scans

the screen. Eventually, she pushes a button on her desktop phone and says: 'Push all my other appointments for this afternoon over to tomorrow, please.' Then she turns to you and says: 'Tell me everything.'

THE DAY AFTER your interview, an officer from the Australian Federal Police flies into Christmas Island. He assures you that they're going to cooperate with police forces overseas to investigate the information on the pen. He counsels you not to talk to anyone from the media or to tell your story online until they've made the bust.

After he leaves, the months drag by. You go to English classes, eat bland food three times a day at the canteen, and go for walks around the perimeter fence with Jamilah to try to slowly build her strength and her lung capacity back up. There is silence from the police. There is no news from Rahama, and Aadan has no more clues.

'I don't want to think this,' he confesses on the phone, 'but we have to face the possibility that maybe she didn't make it. We don't know how strong she was when they dragged her out of the ocean. Jamilah's still the only one who's even seen her.'

More months drag by. After so long of surviving on your wits alone, here you're not even trusted to cook yourself a meal. The boredom and frustration at being so helpless begins to grind you down.

One night, nearly four months into your stay, the news on the TV in the rec room announces that, from now on, asylum seekers who arrive by boat can be taken to remote foreign islands called Nauru and Manus instead of Christmas Island, and never be allowed to enter Australia. You're horrified – if you'd left it a few months later to come to Australia, that could have been you.

Even so, there's still no news about your visa. You feel like the world has forgotten you, left you stranded on this tiny island. The pressure in your chest mounts until you feel like screaming.

You have regular nightmares where Qasim backs you into a corner of a cage, points his finger at you, and sand comes streaming from his fingertip, flowing into your nose and mouth, burying you, until you wake gasping for breath.

Jamilah tells you that she has nightmares too, only hers are about the skeleton of the dead woman in the desert coming to life and nailing her inside a coffin.

Your counsellor, Christine, is a kind woman with bright jewellery. One day, about five months into your stay, she reads you some poems by a woman called Maya Angelou.

'She's also someone who overcame a lot of struggles,' says Christine. The poems are sad, powerful and beautiful. They ease a knot in your soul.

'In English, there's a proverb,' says Christine. 'The pen is mightier than the sword.' As you understand its meaning, a smile spreads over your face.

That night, you have the nightmare again: Qasim's gaunt face; his yellow eyes; the space slipping away from around you as you stumble backwards. He raises his finger, and the storm of sand begins to fly at you.

Then a voice inside you says: *The pen is mightier than the sword.* You reach down to your pocket. Rahama's pen is there. You whip it out and point it at Qasim, and his face drops in horror. He stumbles backwards, cowering. Then you shout the one word that you know will overthrow him forever.

Freedom! you yell, and a blue forcefield blasts out of the tip of the pen. It hurls Qasim into the air with the force of a hurricane. The forcefield clears an open space in front of you, filled with shining blue light.

After you wake up, you feel certain you'll never have that nightmare again.

'QUICK, QUICK!' CRIES Jamilah's voice.

She's running across the grassy oval near the dormitories towards you. It's fantastic how strong and well she seems now.

'Appointment! Immigration! Now!' she shouts, and you jump up and run together to the same beige, boxy room where you first talked to Hilary six months ago.

This time, Hilary's face is glowing with good news. 'Go and pack your things,' she tells you both. 'You have your visas, and we're putting you on the next plane to Melbourne to live with your Uncle Aadan!'

You and Jamilah throw your arms around each other. You whirl her around, nearly knocking over Hilary. You're both cheering and sobbing with delight. Finally, it's over.

When you call Aadan, he's overjoyed. 'I have some more good news,' he tells you.

As soon as he reads the Somali news headline, you know what it means.

'Bright Dream Orphanage Exposed: al-Shabaab's Evil Scheme Busted.'

You whoop and punch the air.

'Now's the time to start writing articles about it for the Australian media,' Aadan tells you. 'We can work on that when you get here.'

That night, you are looking out the window of a plane bound for Melbourne. Jamilah's sleepy head rests on your arm. The stars wink from the deep black sky.

I wonder where Aunty Rahama is right now, you think. *She'd be so proud of us. If she's still alive, I hope the stars that shine on her are lucky ones.*

Your mind goes back to the poem you wrote and left on Christine's desk as a parting gift.

I WILL RISE

A TRIBUTE TO MAYA ANGELOU

You now lock me in detention
And damage my hopes
But that is like dust
And one day I will rise.
You may send me to other countries
And shoot me with your words
But one day I will rise.
You may kill me
With your hateful actions
But that is like air
And one day I will rise.

I may have left a fear-filled life
Full of horror
But one day I will rise.
Does my mind upset you
So full of thoughts?
I am an asylum seeker
who seeks freedom.
I don't have anywhere else to go.
Does it come as a surprise to you
That no matter what
You have done to me
I will forgive you?
Wherever you send me
As long as I see the sun rise
And the moon comes up
I will rise.
I will rise.

✦ To continue with the story, go to page 296.
✦ To read a fact file on Australia's immigration policy, turn to page 321, then return to this page to continue with the story.

You decide to try to swim for the rocks, and you point towards them in an attempt to instruct the woman with the baby to help you kick as hard as she can to help you along. Jamilah is struggling to breathe and can't do any more than cling to the plastic drum.

The woman, though, is scanning the water desperately. 'Husband!' she sobs to you in English. You feel horrified. The water is a churning soup of broken wood and splashing people.

You know, though, that the woman's husband would wish for his wife and baby to survive, so you take her chin, look into her panicked eyes, and say: 'Swim.'

She nods, and you start kicking in the direction of the rocks, somehow all managing to maintain a grip on the slippery plastic drum, the woman also grasping her baby and you grasping Jamilah to ensure neither slips off into the water. Your legs pump as if you're running down the roads of Mogadishu.

The waves try to toss you backwards, but you plough forward. Every so often you glimpse the rocks, but you don't seem to be getting any closer. You turn back towards the wreck and realise you are now a long way from either. You fight down panic.

Your muscles begin to cramp and burn, but you force them to fight on. Jamilah is breathing heavily, and her face is screwed up against the waves. You realise that she is kicking now too – never giving up.

The woman with the baby is having a hard time holding up her child and fighting the weight of her heavy clothes. With a small cry, she loses her grip and slips from the drum.

Instantly, you and Jamilah both let go of the drum and plunge towards her. You manage to get a handful of the woman's clothes and lift her face and her baby's up out of the water. The baby is spluttering and wailing, and you are relieved that he's still alive and strong enough to cry.

'The drum!' shouts Jamilah. The sea has sucked it away from you – you see the moon-white blob of plastic disappear behind a black wave.

'You keep holding her up!' gasps Jamilah. 'I'll get it!' She strikes out for the drum, her arms windmilling, her body rising and falling with the waves.

You kick for all you're worth to keep the woman afloat. She passes you the baby for a moment so that she can rip away her clothes and kick more freely.

You pass back the baby, and look out into the water. There's the plastic drum, even further away now – but where is Jamilah?

You wait for only a split second, but it feels like an eternity, waiting for her head to reappear. When it doesn't, you launch away from the woman and her baby, into the waves after your sister.

It's so hard to swim without anything to grab onto. Your limbs are churning through the water, grasping helplessly. You begin to sink.

Jamilah. With an almighty kick, you manage to break the surface, grab some air, and then flail onwards. The waves push you up, then crush you down. You've lost all sense of direction. Is that white shape the moon, or the drum?

You think you see a pair of shadowy legs kick past you – Jamilah's? – and you make a grasp for them, but they're gone.

You fight, fight, fight. Your chances to snatch a breath get rarer; your limbs seize up in spasms. Water forces its way into your nose, making you choke, and when you gasp involuntarily, a cold flood of water comes rushing in. Your fingers grasp desperately. You look up to see that the waves have closed over your head, and that the star-speckled, choppy surface is drifting further away. Your lungs are burning.

A dream you used to have as a small child flashes in your mind: You dive deep into the ocean at Lido Beach, away from the shore, and sink to the sandy bottom. You think you won't be able to breathe, but you grow gills like a fish and liquid oxygen pours through you. It's as if you've always had the ability to breathe underwater – a dormant connection to a fish-ancestor, which your body has only just remembered. You hear your mum's voice, singing a watery lullaby. The white orb of the moon hangs overhead, with your sister clinging to it.

The ocean pours into your lungs, and your eyes no longer see the moon. As your body drowns, in your mind you simply turn into a fish and swim away. The golden pen in your pocket is now just another shipwreck's treasure.

THE END

✦ To return to your last choice and try again, go to page 254.

You can't go against Aadan's wishes. The boat journey is just too risky – and what might the Australian government *do* in their attempt to appear tougher?

Imagine if you made it to Australia only to be sent back to Indonesia – or Somalia. Imagine if the Australians just decided to send the navy out to torpedo your boats and drown you all.

Aadan says that will never happen, but you grew up in a war zone, so you know it can and it might. You accepted long ago that your life is worthless to anyone who has any power.

You decide to wait, and have faith that you *will* get a visa this way eventually.

A FEW WEEKS later, you and Jamilah are sitting in the kitchen playing cards. A boat left last night, no new people have arrived yet, and Maryam and Majid have gone out shopping, so the only sounds are the *slap*, *slap* of cards and the whine of mosquitoes.

Suddenly the door bangs open and Maryam

staggers into the room. She's clutching her chest, and her face is streaked with tears. You leap to your feet. Jamilah runs to her and holds her hand.

'What is it?' you exclaim. 'Where's Majid?'

At first, Maryam can't even get her words out between shuddering gasps. 'Gone!' she cries eventually. 'Jail!'

You feel a wave of cold horror drench you. The Indonesian police must have arrested Majid for being here without a visa. Maryam is lucky not to have been caught too. Jamilah looks at you in despair.

'*Majid*,' Maryam wails, and her voice swells like a song. '*Majid, Majid, Majid...*'

'He'll be okay, won't he?' Jamilah asks you quietly in Somali.

'I don't know,' you reply.

You've heard stories of the Indonesian jails – they're crowded, violent and filthy. If Majid can't bribe his way out – and you already know that he and Maryam are nearly broke – then he could be trapped for months.

Another sound from Maryam pulls your attention back. It's not just a sob: it's a deep, earthy moan, coming from deep inside. Panting, she holds her belly.

'No,' she whispers. 'No!'

'What's wrong?' you ask. You look into her eyes.

They are wet and bloodshot from tears, and right now they are also wide with fright.

'The baby—' she begins, and then another moan sweeps through her. She staggers backwards against the kitchen wall. Her knees crumple under her.

'Help me catch her!' you shout to Jamilah, and with one of you under each arm, you manage to ease Maryam down the hallway to her and Majid's bedroom.

Maryam drops to her hands and knees on the mattress on the floor, panting loudly. She starts rocking back and forth, keening again: '*Majid...Majid...*'

'I think the baby's coming,' you say to Jamilah in horror. 'What are we going to do? There's no one here to help!'

You're turning back and forth on the spot, panic-stricken. Of all the impossible things you've had to do on this trip, this is the one you feel least prepared for.

'I'm calling Budi,' says Jamilah. 'You...um, I don't know...get some towels or something! And some water.'

Your heart hammers as you run to the kitchen sink and fill a bowl with water. One of your earliest memories is of your hooyo giving birth to Jamilah. You weren't there, of course – but the labour lasted two days and you believed she'd died. In the end, Hooyo lost so much blood that she very nearly did.

Maryam is still on her hands and knees in the bedroom. Her eyes are clenched and her teeth are gritted. You steel yourself and go in. You kneel and dip a towel into the bowl of water, then gently press it to her red face.

The pain seems to subside for a moment, and she looks into your eyes. 'Please,' she whispers, 'help me!'

'Of course I will,' you promise. 'I'm staying right here with you, and it's going to be fine.'

You can only pray that you're right.

Jamilah shouts from the next room: 'Budi says he can find a midwife but we'll have to pay her!'

'Fine!' you shout back. 'But tell him to *hurry*!'

Maryam is swept away by another wave of pain, and your stomach feels like it's full of jumping frogs. *How do women bear this?* you think. *Mothers must be the strongest people Allah ever created.*

The minutes tick into one hour, then two, and still the midwife doesn't arrive. Maryam's moans get deeper, like she's pushing a wheelbarrow of rocks up a mountain.

You go out into the hallway for a quick break, as Jamilah helps Maryam to remove some of her clothes. Blood is pounding in your ears. *What if Maryam dies? What if the baby dies?*

Then a screech comes from the bedroom, like tyres on a wet road. You are at Maryam's side in a flash.

Jamilah shouts, 'You'll have to catch it, quick!'

You can see a little bit of the baby's head, with slick black hair, coming out. Maryam gives a roar that sounds like the earth itself tearing in two, and the baby's whole head appears, facing downwards. Maryam gives a final, heaving yell, you cup your trembling hands, and the baby slips into your arms.

You carefully flip it over. 'You did it!' you shout. 'He's just perfect.' Maryam gives a happy sob.

But something's wrong. The baby is floppy. His skin is purple as a bruise. His little eyes are closed, and he makes no sound.

In that moment, time stands still. There is too much silence. You will him to move, breathe, make a cry. But he just lies still in your arms.

I have to tell Maryam that her baby's dead, you think in horror.

You glance at Jamilah. She is looking at the baby too, stricken. Maryam, still on her hands and knees, can't see her child.

'What's wrong?' she cries. You can't bear to tell her.

Then your mother's voice sounds from somewhere

deep inside you. *Get a towel*, the voice says, *and rub him, gently but vigorously.* You wrap a towel around the gooey, limp body. *Rub, rub, rub.*

Come on, you think, *come on...Allah, please have mercy on Maryam and her baby.*

With a splutter, the baby squeaks and coughs. Instinctively, you roll him over so he's facing the floor again, and you see fluid draining from his little mouth. He chokes, coughs again, then starts to cry in earnest. It's the most beautiful sound you've ever heard.

You let out a sigh of relief bigger than a tidal wave. Warm tears run down your cheeks. You pass the baby boy to Maryam. There is still a cord running from the child's belly to somewhere inside her body, and you hope that's normal, at least for now.

Maryam sits back against the wall, cradling her child, a love-drunk look of triumph and tenderness on her face. Jamilah scoots over to your side and gives you a huge hug.

'We did it!' you cheer. 'I can't believe it!'

'Wow!' is all Jamilah can say. There are tears on her face too.

A few minutes later, Budi finally arrives with the midwife – a wrinkled woman with quick movements and a wispy white bun. She checks over the baby and Maryam, and you go out to the kitchen to have something to eat. When you come back, the midwife shakes your hand firmly in both of hers. She says something in Indonesian.

'Fantastic,' Budi translates into English. 'She says you and Jamilah did a wonderful job.'

You know that the real hero here is Maryam, but, nevertheless, you feel a rush of pride. Maryam passes the baby to Jamilah and wraps you in a strong, warm hug.

'Thank you,' she whispers.

OVER THE NEXT few weeks, then months, the elation fades as Majid fails to come home.

You and Jamilah help as much as you can with baby Mahmoud's baths and nappy changes, but it soon becomes clear that if Majid can't get home soon, Maryam is going to fall apart from worry.

'She barely sleeps,' whispers Jamilah worriedly. 'She barely eats. Mahmoud's nearly two months old now, and she's skin and bones.'

Maryam mostly sits in her darkened room, staring at the wall, holding Mahmoud listlessly. She barely manages to smile or reply when you go in to talk to her.

All the while, travellers come and go from the white house on the hill – although fewer people are arriving, and more are permanently stuck here, since the Australian government started sending asylum seekers to detention centres on remote islands.

'I've had enough,' you tell Jamilah. 'I'm going to get Majid back.'

You've talked about this before, but Maryam and Jamilah have always talked you out of it, because you might never come back.

'You can't!' she cries. 'Please don't. You'll be arrested too!'

'Who *cares*!' you cry back. 'Jamilah, this whole system is just sick. Don't you know that Majid and Maryam ran away from violence just like we did? They didn't have anywhere else to go! They've been here for two-and-a-half years, and just over that ocean out there is Australia, a place we've all nearly died trying to get to, and the best they can do is leave us to rot in Indonesia or send us to some jail on a tiny island. To hell with that! I'm not going to sit here in fear anymore. Get me all the cash we have. Hopefully these jailers will take a bribe.'

Armed with a hefty wad of Indonesian notes, you catch the bus into Jakarta. There, you find a tuktuk driver who speaks good English. He agrees to take you to the jail and, for an extra cost, translate for you.

The jail is a grey, concrete box near the outskirts of town. At the front desk sits a bored-looking man in a green uniform.

'Tell him I'm here to pay bail for the release of Majid Ahmadi,' you say, trying to quell the trembling in your voice.

'He wants to see your papers,' says the tuktuk driver after a brief exchange in Indonesian.

Your heart starts to hammer, but you will yourself to not back down now.

'Tell him I have plenty of paper,' you say, drawing some banknotes from your pocket. Then you put on an even more forceful voice, despite your nerves: 'Now get me Majid Ahmadi. Or I'll find someone else who will.'

The green-uniformed guard regards you for a long while through narrowed brown eyes. At last he replies.

'Bail is fifteen million rupiah,' translates your driver.

That's an astronomical sum – more than this guard would earn in a year. You have two million rupiah in your pocket now, sent by Aadan last week; it's meant to cover rent, food and phone calls for the next few months.

Luckily, the guard is prepared to haggle, and

eventually he gives a curt nod and disappears. You wait for ages, as guards walk by carrying handcuffs and batons, eyeing you suspiciously. Your heart is still racing.

When Majid finally appears, you gasp. He's a walking skeleton – he looks even worse than Maryam. He moves gingerly, as though every movement hurts. But he manages to give you a gleaming smile.

'I HAVE A present for you,' you say to Maryam, standing in the doorway to her darkened room.

When you step back to reveal Majid, she starts giving dry, shaking sobs of disbelief. Majid folds Maryam and Mahmoud into his arms, looking down at his son for the first time. With a lump in your throat, you slip away and leave them to it.

That night, you call Aadan and there's a fire in your belly. You still haven't heard anything back from the UNHCR about your appointment, and it's been six months since you arrived in Indonesia and registered your name with them.

'If I won't get on a boat, and I can't get an appointment with the UNHCR, then I'm trapped in no-man's-land,' you tell him. 'What happened to Majid could just as easily have happened to me, or even to Jamilah. Meanwhile, everything I found out about Bright Dream is gathering dust, while al-Shabaab continues their reign of terror. It's driving me nuts!'

You still carry the pen everywhere in your pocket, but the risks you took to keep it safe have amounted to nothing.

'We talked about this,' says Aadan. 'It's too risky to publish what you know until we can be sure that you, Jamilah and Rahama are in a safe country.'

There's *still* been no sign of Aunty Rahama. The first rush of hope faded long ago, and now you're all trying to fight back the creeping, despairing fear that maybe she didn't make it after all.

You think about the fact that although you've been stuck here for months now, in some ways you've come further than you could have imagined. You saved baby Mahmoud's life, after all, and you brought Majid back to his family.

'I don't care anymore,' you tell Aadan. 'I'm going to go ahead and put the story out there.'

Despite his protests, you go down to the internet cafe the next day and spend hours writing your story. Then with Majid's help, you attach all the files on the pen and email it to the major Kenyan, Somali and international news agencies.

You know news of your location might filter back to al-Shabaab if the story's published, and you know it's possible they'll have related terrorist gangs here in Indonesia they could use to target you. Nevertheless, you're ready to strike your final blow to this monster that's been shadowing you ever since the bomb blast at the broadcasting building in Mogadishu.

You punch 'send' and close your eyes in triumph.

A FEW DAYS tick by with no reply. Then, suddenly, your phone and email start running hot. One agency picked up the story, the others caught the scent, and it has now snowballed into a major news item.

One call is different from the rest – it's the UNHCR office in Jakarta, where your papers were registered all those months ago. They want you and Jamilah to come into the office as soon as possible.

When the two of you get there, the waiting room is as crowded as before, but this time an Indonesian woman comes to fetch you. She has a long black ponytail and poppy-red lipstick, and the nametag on her crisp white shirt says 'Rika'.

In Rika's air-conditioned office, a beefy man with a sunburnt nose is sitting in a chair that's too small for him. He rises to greet you with a handshake.

'Barry Mackenzie,' he says in English. 'From Interpol – the international police.'

You're not sure what to say.

'So,' he goes on, 'you're the young journo who's been making these claims, eh? Orders from head office were to come and check it out.'

'I haven't done anything wrong…have I?' you ask.

Are you in trouble? You glance at Jamilah. She shrugs, looking worried.

'No, nothing like that, not at all. You've done a good thing, son. Could be the information we need to track down some of these bast— ahem, *criminal suspects* once and for all.'

He asks to see the pen, which by now is famous from being described in all the news reports. He whistles, impressed, as you draw it from your pocket.

You're reluctant to hand it over. 'I've been through so much for this pen,' you murmur. 'But we still haven't got it to safety in Australia.'

Barry nods slowly. 'Indonesia's not the safest place for a pair of kids, particularly ones with a bent for stirring up hornet's nests,' he agrees.

He leans towards Rika and murmurs in her ear. She considers a moment, then begins tapping at her keyboard.

'All we want is a visa so we can live with our Uncle Aadan in Australia,' says Jamilah.

You nod, then add boldly: 'And we won't leave this office until we're sure we have your protection.'

'Can you step out to the waiting room, please?' asks Rika sharply, not looking up from her computer. You're worried you've blown it, but Barry gives you a wink as you leave the room.

After an hour of waiting, you and Jamilah are called back one at a time and asked to tell Barry and Rika your story in detail. Then you're sent back to the waiting room, for a further six hours.

The waiting room is empty and night has fallen when at last Rika and Barry emerge, looking browbeaten but satisfied.

'We did it,' says Barry. 'Pulled every string I could for you kids.'

'What did you do?' you ask with bated breath. You don't dare to hope they might have pulled off the impossible...

'Two emergency rescue visas,' says Rika proudly. 'And a flight to Melbourne that leaves in the morning!'

Jamilah drops to her knees. You start to sob.

'Thank you,' you manage to say, though these two words are not enough to cover your overwhelming gratitude.

We're saved! We can live with Aadan. We're going to be okay.

In the next moment, you realise you'll be leaving Maryam, Majid and Mahmoud to their neverending hell, and your shoulders begin to shake as grief rises up to mingle with your joy.

THE NEXT MORNING, you lean your face against the cold window inside the plane. Jamilah sits beside you, gazing into the distance with a dreamy, sad smile.

Saying goodbye to your beloved friends and their baby was agony. As you watch the sun rise through the clouds, you think of the poem you wrote last night, and pressed into Majid's hands first thing this morning as a parting gift.

TO THE ONES I LEFT BEHIND

The pain and suffering that you are all going
    through,
I didn't forget.
The guerrilla war and the loss of your loved ones,
I didn't forget.
The mothers who lost their sons and husbands,
I didn't forget.
The boys and girls that were mistreated,
I didn't forget.
The breaking up of families, unable to
    communicate,
I didn't forget.
The enemies who killed all the important people,

I didn't forget.
Our home that turned into fire,
I didn't forget.
Our civilians who were forgotten in the refugee
*   camps,*
I didn't forget.
The ones who are going by boats and risking
*   their lives,*
I didn't forget.
The ones held in detention for uncountable
*   months,*
I didn't forget.
The children with no one to care about their
*   education or future,*
I didn't forget.
My dear mother and father, aunty and friends,
I didn't forget you either.
One day I will come back and change our home
*   with my knowledge.*
Thank you, New Country, for giving me a
*   chance to live again.*
I'm a child of Africa, but I will be a man of
*   Australia.*

✦ To continue with the story, go to page 296.

The next time Budi visits the white house on the hill, you tell him you're ready to leave, as soon as possible.

When the evening of your departure comes, Maryam gives you bags laden with her favourite Iranian dishes.

Majid grips your forearm in a brother's handshake and pulls you into a hug. 'You saved my sister's life,' you tell him.

Jamilah embraces Maryam, then plants a little kiss on her round belly.

Everyone is wiping away tears.

At the coast, you smell the sea before you reach it, briny and crisp. Your stomach bubbles with anticipation. The smell takes you back to the shores of Lido Beach, home in Mogadishu.

This ocean is no different, you tell yourself. *Don't be scared. Just one more trip, and we'll be in Australia.*

IN BRIGHTLY LIT living rooms across Australia, headlines blare on the evening news.

Flood of asylum seekers: number of boat arrivals reaches record high.

One hundred and fifty-four boat people drowned at sea so far this year.

Stop the boats.

THE BOAT RIDE is a terrible nightmare.

You're on a fishing boat suited to twenty or so people, with nearly one hundred aboard. The waves bounce and heave. Children whimper, and the engine revs with its heavy load. Your face is crusted with salt spray; your stomach churns. Jamilah clings to you, crying. You vomit over the side, your clothes soaked with acidic yellow spew – again and again. You pray it will be over soon.

THERE'S NO SHADE. Your head throbs. Your skin is tight. Your sleep is black, dreamless. Others on board are kind to you, and you are weak with gratitude. And still it is not over.

THE SKY BURNS bright-blue. The air is oddly quiet. The waves slap the hull.

There is no engine noise.

The engine's dead. You're just drifting.

IN AUSTRALIA, THE headlines blare on.

Labor has lost control of Australia's borders.

More riots feared at Villawood Detention Centre.

Stop the boats.

THERE'S NO MEASURE of how far you've drifted, where in the ocean you are; blue sky and blue sea blur into a blinding, endless whole. There are no flares, no radio to signal for help. There is no food, and not enough water left.

You'd sooner throw yourself overboard and drown than die agonisingly of thirst.

The sun sizzles your skin. The salt makes you burn and itch madly. Jamilah is unconscious. *If I jump overboard to escape this hell, will I take her with me?*

And still it goes on.

YOU ARE RESCUED by the Australian navy. Through your weakness and your pain, you feel a huge bubble of triumph rise inside you. People all around you are sobbing with joy and giving prayers of thanks.

When the navy ship is close enough, smaller dinghies launch from the big ship. A uniformed navy officer with a square chin and kind blue eyes helps you and Jamilah onto his smaller craft. You shake his hand and offer your thanks.

You've truly been saved. Relief washes over you. *All the risks we took*, you think, *and all the decisions we had to make were worth it. We survived.*

But you thought too soon. They aren't planning to take you to safety at all.

POLICE FOIL ANOTHER *Islamic terrorist bomb threat*, scream the headlines.

Pacific Island detention centres to be reopened.

'That'll teach them,' say the mums and the dads in Australia, satisfied. 'Teach them that they can't come here illegally.'

Stop the boats.

Stop the boats.

Stop the boats.

YOU ARE SEPARATED from Jamilah. She is taken to a detention centre on Christmas Island, which is part of Australia, but you are sent to Nauru. This one little island is its own country, not part of Australia. *Nauru.* You never even knew it existed. Maybe the rest of the world doesn't know it exists either.

In Nauru, there is nothing to sleep in but stifling hot army tents. There is white shale rock underfoot, and wire fences encircle the camp.

You are frantic with worry. *Why can't I be with my sister? When can I go to Australia?* All the other asylum seekers here seem to be adult men, although there are a couple who look young, like you.

'I don't think I'm meant to be here,' you try explaining to the staff. 'I'm not an adult. I'm only fourteen. I need to be with my sister!'

The staff say they'll look into it, but then they rush off to the next crisis, and you never hear back from them. You only hear rumours from the other men that the law has changed, Australia is trying to keep boat arrivals out, and you might be here forever.

They can't keep me here forever! you think. *Australians are good people, and they have fair laws. They wouldn't let this happen.*

Yet all around you come the sounds of hasty construction, as the contractors struggle to get the detention centre ready for hundreds more refugees yet to arrive.

THERE IS ONE staff member here who seems to want to get to know you. His name is Mark, and he works for the Salvation Army. He says that the database here has you listed as eighteen years old. He's frustrated because he can't get any of his superiors to admit that there's been a mistake.

'I have to get out of here,' you tell him. 'I have to get my family back together. One day, I want to be a journalist. I want to bring down al-Shabaab!'

I need freedom, you think, day and night. You thirst for it, as badly as you longed for water when you walked out of Dadaab. *I can't reach any of my dreams if I don't have freedom.*

You write a poem and give it to Mark the next day.

FREEDOM FOR EDUCATION
Born in endless war
Searching for food inside a gun
Poor people die.
What I have seen stays in my memories.
Growing up in such hard life
With no rights for young or old.
Learning is filled with fears.
Just knowing education is best.
Day and night fight
That is my home

All I have known
Where I got grown
The world is full of lessons.
Out of the darkness
I have come the farthest.
Among the hardest
We survived
Arrived
In a peace-full world
But I heard them say
We send them to Nauru
That is what they say.
That was their answer.
I need freedom to forget the past.
We need freedom,
A chance to learn,
Not to be returned
To face death.
We patiently wait.
When will we be free?
Is the beautiful day far away?
With pain-full words I say:
Give us a visa.
Look at our situations.
Imagine our problems.
Everyone needs freedom.

Mark takes your poem and reads it thoughtfully. The next day, he reappears.

'I put your poem up on my Facebook page,' he says. 'It's going gangbusters. Seven hundred shares already!'

Mark has to explain to you what 'Facebook', 'gangbusters' and 'seven hundred shares' mean before you understand that people are reading your poem. Hundreds of people, whom you've never met. People who vote. Australian people.

If the government sent you to Nauru because the Australian people wanted it, couldn't they bring you to Australia if the people change their minds? You ask Mark.

'It's complicated,' he says.

The very next day, Mark tells you that he was nearly sacked for posting your poem online, so he won't be able to do it again.

But he's shown you that your words have power. You just have to keep getting them out there, somehow, any way you can, and maybe one day they'll get *you* out of here, too.

AS THE WEEKS drag by, Nauru begins to feel more and more like a pot with a heavy lid on it – nearly bursting with frustration and heat.

Some of the men in the camp hold a protest, but

you're afraid to join in. You don't know what they do to troublemakers here. Could it damage your chances for a visa? Do you even *have* a chance for a visa? Why won't anyone tell you the truth?

You are hiding in a tent nearby. You hear a man with a megaphone make an announcement to the protesters.

'Nobody is forcing you to stay here. If you wish to return to your own country, the Australian government will pay for your flight home.'

His words are met with howls of derision and anger. Slowly, they begin to sink into your mind.

You imagine being flown back to Mogadishu, and beginning the cat-and-mouse game with al-Shabaab all over again.

This man obviously has no idea what any of you are facing, should you return.

And suddenly, you understand – really understand. You're trapped.

THE END

✦ To return to your last decision and try again, go to page 242.

'It's been a long path, from Mogadishu to Melbourne,' you say. You look down at your hands resting on the speaker's lectern. They are the hands of a young man.

These hands hold steering wheels and microphones; they press buttons in lifts and type a hundred words per minute. But they are still the same hands that carried a gun across the desert; wiped the sweat from Jamilah's brow; installed plastic-bottle lights in Dadaab; gripped the deck of a boat, and the sides of a truck, on your quest for freedom.

The screen behind you on the stage shows the cover of your book, *From Mogadishu to Melbourne*, featuring the cover of those same hands again – yours – holding Aunty Rahama's golden pen.

'There were so many times that my life was in danger,' you say. You are speaking to a packed high school assembly. Hundreds of faces watch you in amazement. Your story is unlike anything they've heard before.

'Al-Shabaab – that's the terrorist group that controlled much of Somalia and is still a terrible threat today – wanted me dead. But there were two things I had to live for: my sister, Jamilah, and this pen.'

You take the golden pen from your pocket. Your audience knows this part of the story, because it made international headlines. With the exposure of Bright Dream, hundreds of orphans destined for the frontlines of al-Shabaab's dirty war were rescued and given true hope. And the money trail in the bank account left a clear set of footprints for the investigators to follow: who al-Shabaab had bought their weapons from; in what towns they had conducted transactions or built hide-outs; which vehicles were purchased and what kind of technology they had for surveillance and attack.

With this treasure-trove of information, the AMISOM forces conducted a series of major raids, bringing down a major military leader of al-Shabaab and dozens of unit commanders. The movement is still alive, but significantly weakened, with al-Shabaab one step closer to defeat and Somalia one step closer to peace, thanks to your efforts in bringing this crucial information out safely.

When you conclude your talk, the audience gives you a standing ovation. You take some questions from the eager crowd.

'You said the pen has an interesting history – can you tell us about that?' asks a boy.

'Absolutely,' you say. 'Well, the story goes that back in 1825, an Irish convict brought a special bracelet to Australia, sewn into the hem of her skirt. The bracelet contained seven gems, and the first letter of each gem spelt out a word – in this case "F" for fire opal, "R" for ruby and so on, spelling the seven-letter word "freedom".

'The bracelet broke and the gems were shared. The ruby went to a man named "Inky" Williams, who was my Uncle Aadan's great-great-great-great-grandfather! Of course, Aadan added the memory stick himself, to give as a gift to my Aunty Rahama,' you add. 'The other six freedom gems could be anywhere. But this pen brought me my freedom, because it gave me a reason to write and to speak up.'

A field of hands shoot up with further questions. 'There's time to answer one more,' you say, and pick out a girl in the front row.

'What are you going to do next?' she asks.

'Well,' you reply, 'you remember how I actually met some of the orphans from Bright Dream by accident when my sister and I hitched a lift out of the desert? At the time, I was sure they'd all be killed in an al-Shabaab mission before too long. But I've just been contacted by Hassan!'

The audience gasps, delighted.

'Yeah. I know. I was so excited to hear it too. And now Hassan wants to go back to Somalia and start a *real* orphanage to help all the kids who were mistreated by Bright Dream.

'He's in Kenya at the moment. I'm flying there next month to interview him, before he returns to Somalia to start the new orphanage, and I'm hoping to use the money I raise here in Australia from my book sales and talks to support him.

'I also want to visit my friends in Kenya who you read about in the book – Sampson and Abshir in Nairobi, and Jok and Adut, who still live in Dadaab. I also want to raise funds for Maryam and Majid; they're still stuck in Indonesia until Australia starts accepting visa applications from there again, but they want to start a school there for refugee kids like their son, Mahmoud.

'But that's my long-term plan. In the short term, once I'm finished talking to you guys, I have a birthday party to go to. Thanks for being such a great audience!'

The principal shakes your hand warmly and you hurry from the hall into the summer afternoon sunshine – you don't want to be late for the party. When you get to Aadan's house, Jamilah is already there in the living room, lounging on the couch. She looks so smart in her school uniform. You can't believe she's fourteen years old already!

But the guest of honour still isn't here...

'Where is she?' you ask Jamilah. 'She can't be late for her own birthday party!'

'Oh, you know her,' says Jamilah and laughs. 'She takes forever in the shower!'

Just then, a breath of hot air and sweet-smelling shampoo wafts into the living room as a figure walks in, a towel around her head. She gives her frizzy hair one last rub and throws the damp towel back, and you see that wonderful face – the face of the woman who hid with you in a hole in the ground, who faked her own death to trick the terrorists, who Jamilah saw on the TV as she was dragged from the ocean; the face of the woman who managed to save all your lives. Aunty Rahama.

You run to her and she squeezes you into a hug as if you were still a little boy, although by now her head fits under your chin. She takes your hand and limps to the table. The doctors have said she'll always have that limp, a legacy of the stroke she had after she was pulled from the ocean, which kept her in a coma in an Italian hospital all that time you were searching for her.

Aadan comes in from the kitchen carrying two amazing-smelling platters of food – Somali and Australian dishes, all Aunty Rahama's favourites, a feast to rival the amazing wedding party they held three years ago for all their family and friends.

When you hug Rahama now, you notice how you have to bend around her growing baby bump. She and Aadan are expecting a little boy in the autumn. They are thinking of naming him Zayd.

Zayd stayed by Aunty Rahama's side in Italy the whole time she was unconscious, never giving up hope, trying every way he knew to try to trace you, until she eventually regained consciousness and told him how to contact Aadan. He now lives in Germany and works as a taxi driver.

Jamilah is in the doorway now, hissing your name. You follow her to the kitchen.

'Here – sign Aunty Rahama's card,' she says.

You always keep the Freedom Pen in your shirt pocket – it's both a good-luck charm and a badge of honour to you. You pull it out now, and write in Rahama's birthday card: *To Rahama, you make my heart come alive.*

You still write poems with the golden pen, too – although you're now studying to become a qualified journalist, you still have a heart full of poetry. The book you've just published ends with the words:

I write because my tongue has no bones
But it's strong enough to break down all the
haters' words.

You and Jamilah are called to the table – it's time to feast! A circle of raised glasses catch the light, and three smiling faces turn to you: your family. A kookaburra laughs in the garden, and the sunset turns the steam from the feast golden.

'To freedom!' says Rahama.

It's the same toast she makes – you all make – every time you sit down together, but you never grow tired of it. It's a family song you all know the words to. It reminds you of everything you've been blessed with.

'To freedom,' you reply.

THE END

FACT FILE:
SOMALIA

Somalia is a country on the north-eastern coast of Africa. It's shaped like the number '7', with the long part of the '7' adjoining the Indian Ocean. It is home to 14.3 million people, most of whom are Sunni Muslims, and its capital is Mogadishu.

These days, when you mention Somalia or Mogadishu, most people think of war and famine. But it wasn't always like that. Records show that as far back as when the ancient Egyptians were building their pyramids, they were trading commodities such as gold, wood and ivory with those from the rich southern 'Land of Punt', which historians think was around the area of present-day Somalia. Mogadishu was such a beautiful city that for many years it was known as 'the White Pearl of the Indian Ocean'.

As European countries became more powerful in the 1800s, though, they weren't going to leave this African treasure-trove untouched. Italy and Britain colonised (took over) Somalia, and controlled it for nearly a hundred years, from the late 1800s until 1960.

After Somalia gained independence from the colonisers, there was a brief period of peace until, in 1969, a dictator* called Siad Barre seized power. Eventually, more than twenty years later in 1991, Barre's government collapsed and Somalia was left without a leader, which threw the country into chaos as different would-be leaders fought for power.

The civil war – a type of war where a country fights within itself – began in 1991 and continues in some parts of the country today.

In 2006, a radical Islamic terrorist group called al-Shabaab joined the struggle for control of Somalia. At the time this story opens, in early September 2011, Mogadishu is protected by AMISOM†. However, al-Shabaab still controlled much of the countryside and sometimes mounted attacks in central Mogadishu, hoping to overthrow it. Today, al-Shabaab continues to represent a significant threat to peace in Somalia. A truck bomb in Mogadishu in 2017 killed 512 people. The history of clan-based conflict in Somalia makes it difficult for the country to unite against al-Shabaab.

---

* A leader who rules the country by force, and is not chosen as leader by the people.

† The African Union Mission in Somalia, a peacekeeping force made up of soldiers from other African countries, with a mission to stabilise Somalia.

This continuing conflict, and ongoing droughts and famine in the region, mean that every day, Somali people still face huge hurdles to making a living, or accessing healthcare or education.

Despite its turbulent history, Somali people love their country and their culture. Somali people say that they love to laugh, that their cooking is the best in the world, and that they have a strong sense of family and community spirit. There is so much more to know and understand about Somalia – and, luckily for Australia, over 6000 Somalis now live here, and many of them are happy to share their history and culture.

✦ Return to page 20 to make your choice.

FACT FILE:
JOURNALISTS AT RISK

Have you ever stayed quiet about something that was bothering you, because you were worried you'd get into trouble if you spoke up? Or have you ever told the truth even though you knew someone else would be angry at you for doing so?

These are the kinds of problems journalists face all the time. If a journalist finds evidence of a powerful person cheating or lying, they'll probably feel it's important for the public to know the truth, even though that powerful person will be angry about being exposed. Or if a journalist writes an opinion piece that expresses an unpopular view, they might be criticised for saying what they think.

In Australia, we have laws to protect journalists, and to protect the people who are interviewed by journalists. Journalists have 'freedom of speech', which is a human right to say or publish what you wish without fear. But there are also laws to protect people from journalists who go too far – for example, journalists aren't allowed to publish 'hate speech' or anything that unfairly attacks someone or damages their reputation. There is a delicate balance between these two sets of laws.

In some countries, these laws either don't exist, or they are ignored. This makes being a journalist very risky - especially if they publish a truth that a powerful person or group wants to keep secret. Journalists might be jailed, threatened or even killed for doing this[‡]. When the media is controlled in this way, the public are kept in the dark; instead of the truth, they are told lies by the people who have the power and money to control what is published.

Somalia is one of the worst countries in the world for journalists' freedom. Reporters are often in fear of their lives, especially if they report on problems within the government or al-Shabaab. A few brave journalists continue to take great risks because they are passionate about freedom of speech.

Would you put your life on the line to broadcast the truth?

✤ Return to page 34 to make your choice.

[‡] The Reporters without Borders website shows that every year, there are 80–100 media workers killed worldwide for doing their job, and that (as of mid-2017) there are nearly 400 media workers worldwide in jail just for speaking out.

FACT FILE:
RELIGIOUS EXTREMISM

Every religion has radical groups, or extremists. These are the people who believe it's all right to kill or hurt other people in the name of their religion, and who believe that every person in the world should be forced to follow their faith.

No religion is free from extremists. For example, although Buddhism and Hinduism have reputations as being peaceful religions, extremists from both groups often carry out deadly attacks in India, Sri Lanka and other Asian nations. Christian extremism is also on the rise, particularly in the United States.

However, almost all people who follow any religion are *not* extremists. Most people are happy to coexist with other religions and would never claim that their god wants them to carry out acts of violence. This is true of all religions, including the huge majority of Muslim people. On the news in Western countries, we currently see a lot about Islamic (or Muslim) extremism. Some people therefore mistakenly believe that all Muslims are potential terrorists. This has led to a rise in racist attacks against peaceful

Muslim people, which only creates deeper divisions in our society and entrenches misunderstandings.

It is important that we are on guard in Australia to prevent any terrorist[§] attacks from being carried out here, and to make sure no Australian people become violent extremists. However, we should not feel fearful of all people from another country just because an extremist group operates there. Remember that most people are not extremists, and most refugees are running *away* from terrorists – they are not terrorists themselves.

There are many quotes in the Muslim holy book, the Qur'an, that condemn violence and encourage us to live peacefully together. Nearly all imams (Muslim religious leaders) condemn terrorism and extremism as being the opposite to what Allah (God) and his Prophet Mohammed would have wanted. The same is true of all the other religions' holy books and leaders.

When we make friends and build bridges of understanding between different cultures, we make it harder for extremism to take root.

✳ Go to page 46 to continue with the story.

§ Groups or individuals who use violence to make a political or religious point.

FACT FILE:
Crossing Borders 'Illegally'

To cross an international border legally you need identity documents, such as a passport and visa[¶]. But people running for their lives often don't have time to organise a visa – and if their government is corrupt, at war or discriminating against them, that government won't give them a passport. Furthermore, it is only possible to apply for refugee status after you've crossed an international border – you can't apply within your own country.

When people cross a border without these papers, this is sometimes described as them entering the new country 'illegally'. But people running to safety just need to get across the border any way they can.

The United Nations (UN) knows this. In 1951, at the end of the Second World War, they established the UNHCR (United Nations High Commission for Refugees) to manage the flow

[¶] A passport proves your identity and citizenship of your home country; a visa states your permission to enter the new country and for how long you may stay.

of refugees worldwide. Participating countries made an agreement about the rights of refugees, including the right to seek asylum (a safe place). That means that if you are running for your life, it's not illegal to cross a border without the required documents. Just like an ambulance can break the speed limit and not be fined, a person seeking safety can cross a border without documents and not be fined, because in both cases, they have a special reason to break the law - they are trying to save a life.

✳ Return to page 89 to make your choice.

FACT FILE:
REFUGEES AND ASYLUM SEEKERS

An asylum seeker is someone who crosses an international border and claims to be in danger. These claims are heard by the UNHCR or the government of the host country, and if the person is found to be in need of protection, they are defined as a 'refugee'**.

Refugees are not always poor, and they can come from any country in the world. In their host countries, they may live in camps or in cities. What they have in common is that they didn't *want* to leave their home, but felt they had to so they could survive.

There are lots of situations that can push someone into being a refugee, but the most common one is war. That means the countries who host the greatest number of refugees are the neighbours of countries at war. For example, in 2015, 2.5 million

** If it is decided that an asylum seeker is not in need of protection, they may be sent back to their own country, but this is a very complicated legal process.

refugees (that's about one in every ten people in Australia) fled a war in Syria to Turkey next door, and Ethiopia received 736,100 refugees, many from its neighbour Somalia.

Refugees may have a lot to offer their host country: they may have useful skills or qualifications; they may be hard-working and determined. But refugees may also have pressing health needs, as well as basic human needs such as shelter, food and water, and host countries may struggle to meet these needs if many refugees arrive at once.

How can the countries of the world best cooperate to support and appreciate refugees?

✦ Go to page 112 to continue with the story.

FACT FILE:
BOTTLE-LIGHTS AND OTHER GREAT INVENTIONS

Sometimes the best inventions are the simplest. In a place like a refugee camp, which struggles to meet people's basic needs, a simple invention can have life-changing consequences. Often it's the people who live in these difficult circumstances themselves who come up with the best ideas.

The bottle-light from the story is a real invention. It was invented by Alfredo Moser, a Brazilian mechanic. During his city's frequent electricity blackouts, he came up with a simple solution: to use a bottle of water, fitted into a hole in the roof, to refract the sun's light and illuminate a room.

A charity picked up on his idea and trained people to make and install them, and now Moser's bottle-lights light up more than 350,000 homes without electricty in over fifteen countries around the world!

It's not only Moser who is finding ways to bring great simple ideas to people who need them most. Ann Makosinski, a fifteen-year-old Canadian schoolgirl, invented the first ever torch that doesn't need batteries or solar panels and instead runs on just the heat of your body. When the torch touches your skin, it lights up.

There are lots more simple and amazing inventions out there, which you can research yourself. Maybe someday you will invent one too!

People all over the world need shelter, sanitation, clean water, education, and many more necessities that are basic human rights. Most inventors spend their time making things like the latest-model phones or heated leather car seats, because expensive, fancy inventions make people rich. But simple, effective inventions can save lives.

Alfredo Moser never became rich from the bottle-light, but he has a huge sense of pride about it. 'I'd never have imagined [it would help so many],' he said in an interview. 'It gives you goose-bumps to think about[††].

✷ Return to page 123 to continue with the story.

[††] Alfredo Moser in 'Bottle Light Inventor Proud to Be Poor', by Gibby Zobel, BBC World Service, Uberaba, Brazil, *BBC News Magazine*, 13 August 2013. http://www.bbc.com/news/magazine-23536914

FACT FILE:
PEOPLE SMUGGLERS

A 'people smuggler' is someone who helps other people to cross a border in secret without the required documents. People smugglers may or may not be paid for the work they do.

People smugglers might be trying to help you, or they might be criminals who just want to make money from desperate people seeking safety. They might be reliable and get you safely across the border, or they might take your money and run, leaving you to your fate. They might even sell you as a slave, or hold you hostage until your relatives give them more money. Because of these risks, it is very, very scary to put your life in a people smuggler's hands.

Desperate people use people smugglers. Often a whole family will sell everything they own just to get one member to safety. They risk a dangerous journey because their home is even more dangerous, and a safe option to escape is not available to them.‡‡

‡‡ Those who can't afford a people smuggler may end up killed, or living as 'internally displaced people', which means they live like refugees within their own country.

Millions of people around the world have either been sent to their deaths or had their lives saved by a people smuggler. If your grandparents escaped Europe during World War II, or if your parents came to Australia at the end of the Vietnam War, maybe *you* are only reading these words right now thanks to them trusting their lives to a people smuggler.

If we could do these three things, then refugees would not need to use people smugglers so much:

1. Make refugees' home countries peaceful.
2. Give the neighbouring countries extra support so refugees can build new lives there.
3. Make visas and transport to Western countries much more readily available.

It will take a lot of time, goodwill and dedication to achieve those three things, but it can be done.

✦ Return to page 189 to make your choice.

FACT FILE:
LIFE IN LIMBO

All over the world, asylum seekers and refugees live in countries like Malaysia, Kenya, Turkey, Indonesia, and many others. These countries give limited protection and opportunities for refugees, and visas to resettle in Western countries are so rare that most refugees will never get one. Unable to go home, unable to reach a country that will give them full citizenship, these refugees may spend the rest of their lives 'in limbo'.

Imagine living in a country where it was illegal for you to work, where you couldn't ever go to school, where you might be sent to jail at any time for just being in the country, and where you couldn't go to a hospital if you got sick. How would you survive? How would you make a future for your children in such a place? This is the reality of life for thousands of refugees and asylum seekers around the world.

Even some asylum seekers who live in Australia feel as though they are in 'limbo' here while they wait for the government to hear their case and grant them a permanent visa.

It may seem strange, but many host countries actually don't want to offer laws and services that would make life easier for refugees, because they don't want to encourage too many refugees to come there.

Many countries would prefer to make it safe for refugees to return to their own countries instead – but to do this, we would have to make a huge global effort to eradicate all famine and war. Can it be done?

In the future, because of climate change, it's possible that we will also have 'climate refugees' who can never return home because their homes are underwater, or stricken by never-ending drought. No country currently has any laws to deal with 'climate refugees', because it hasn't happened yet.

How can we do our share to help and to be a world leader in the future?

✦ Return to page 242 to make your choice.

FACT FILE:
AUSTRALIA'S IMMIGRATION POLICY

Every country has the right to make its own laws about who to let into their country, how many people can come, and who can go on to be offered citizenship of that country. These are called a country's immigration laws.

In Australia, there's a big debate about whether we should take more, or fewer, refugees than we do (between 13,000 and 20,000 per year from 2010 to 2017). Some say we can't afford it and should take less; others say it's our duty as a wealthy country to help more of those in need. Long-term studies show that refugees usually do lots of good in their new homes – bringing new culture and generating money of their own – but some Australians fear people different to them will 'take over'.

Imagine you have control over immigration into Australia. There are 65.3 million people without a safe home who would like to live here – nearly three times as many people as Australia's entire population. How many refugees will you let in – and how will you decide who gets to come first? This is a thorny problem that even the world's greatest leaders can't solve.

Some refugees are given a visa for Australia before they arrive. Other asylum seekers come without a visa, and although they have a legal right to seek safety, in 1992 Australia started holding asylum seekers in detention centres in Australia while their claims were processed. In 2001, Australia introduced a new law: to send asylum seekers to offshore detention.

Australia set up two offshore detention centres: one on Nauru (a tiny island in the Pacific), and another on Manus Island (in Papua New Guinea). The centres are intended to put people off attempting to reach Australia by boat - by showing them they will be sent to an offshore detention centre instead if they try.

Both major political parties have sent asylum seekers, including children, to offshore detention in the years since 2001. Sometimes teenage boys have been mistaken for adult men and detained with the adults for some time; this happens in one of the scenes in this book. Hundreds of asylum seekers have been held in offshore detention for years, with no hope of reaching a safe country, and still too afraid to go home. Waiting in limbo, under immense mental pressure, without decent medical care or education, has driven many asylum seekers to despair.

Meanwhile, at the time this book went to print (January 2018), the government has also cut hundreds of millions of dollars from Australia's foreign-aid budget, and greatly reduced the numbers of humanitarian visas Australia offers to those waiting in refugee camps overseas and in 'transit' countries like Malaysia and Indonesia.

While some people are pleased that Australia's policies are keeping asylum seekers out, others claim that we have turned our backs on those in need. But 'tough' immigration policies only exist because they seem popular with the voting Australian public.

Are these laws popular with you? If not, how are you going to let the government know about it? And what do you think should be the alternative to the 'Pacific Solution'?

✳ Return to page 266 to continue with the story.

FACT FILE:
INTERVIEW WITH HANI ABDILE

Hani Abdile is a poet and an asylum seeker who travelled alone from Somalia to Australia when she was only seventeen years old. Many of the scenes in this book are based on Hani's memories, and the poems on pages 122-123, 265-266, 285-286, 292-293 and 302 are written by her.

EMILY: Hani, the first question I want to ask you is: What does freedom mean to you?

HANI: Freedom means a lot to me. If freedom could be a person, I would like to be her slave.

EMILY: What do you think freedom means when you're an asylum seeker?

HANI: I think freedom means everything for every individual. It doesn't matter what kind of situation they are in. It's just something that you really need in your life.

Sometimes in the Christmas Island detention centre, I used to feel like I didn't have the freedom to think, you know? Even when you go outside [in the yards or on excursion] there, you're kind of free because you can walk around, but you're actually only free physically, not mentally, because you have so much stress about your future.

⊷————⊷

EMILY: That's an interesting distinction – to be free, you need to have both physical and mental freedom. Do you think it's possible that if somebody takes away your freedom physically you can still have your mental freedom?

HANI: Yeah, I think if you fight for it. Sometimes it's better to be physically imprisoned rather than mentally imprisoned. Because when you have a physical lack of freedom, you know that, 'Oh, I can't walk here, I can't get out of here.' That you know. But when you are mentally locked up but you are physically free, that is the worst, because you don't know what your future holds, or when you will be mentally free. Freedom doesn't mean just walking free, it also means being free mentally, emotionally, and, you know – everything.

EMILY: Can you tell me how far you would go for freedom, or maybe tell me some of the things that you've already done that demonstrate how far you would go for freedom?

HANI: For freedom, I would touch the sun. I would touch the sun even though it's too hot. Yeah, because for me, freedom means a lot. As I told you, if freedom was a person, I could be her slave for the rest of my life. Because without freedom, life is just...you know, life is impossible. You can keep living life without freedom, but it wouldn't be as sweet as it is with freedom.

EMILY: So, in the book, the characters have to make a lot of choices that influence their freedom. Can you give me an example of some of the choices that you've made?

HANI: The choices that I've made to be free... well, for me, I travelled miles and miles to get the freedom that I needed. But then living in the Christmas Island detention centre was not the perfect place, even though I had most of the things that I needed.

To get that freedom, I had to do lot of things that upset me. But I also found that the weapon that could bring me that freedom was my ability to write and to speak up.

———————

EMILY: Were there many times on your journey when you felt like you didn't have any choice in what happened next?

HANI: Yeah. So, when the guy nailed me under the boat deck as if I was a dead person, I knew that I didn't have any choice. But it got me the freedom I wanted, and I think nothing ever comes easy in the world – you have to fight for it.

Every time I think about freedom, I will always remember Nelson Mandela, who spent twenty years behind bars and fought for the freedom of the rest of the South African people. He was just a person like me, you know? He had a brain, and he had everything that I have. He didn't have anything extra, but with patience and willpower, it got him through all those hard times.

So, it didn't matter to me how many walls were in front of me to reach my freedom – I knew that I would fight for it until my last breath.

————◆————

✳ Return to page 123 to continue with the story.

STORIES ABOUT SOMALI REFUGEES, BY SOMALI REFUGEES

Video of Hani telling her story and
reading poems:
https://www.youtube.com/watch?v=fbRn26mikJg,
Hani Abdile, 'Living Library', MerJa Media,
Australia, 16 September 2015

Book of poetry (for adults):
I Will Rise, by Hani Abdile, Writing Through
Fences, Australia, 2016.

Inspirational schools speaker link for
Abdi Aden:
Booked Out, Australia, http://bookedout.com.
au/find-a-speaker/author/abdi-aden/

Memoir (for adults):
Shining: The Story of a Lucky Man, by Abdi
Aden with Robert Hillman, Harper Collins,
Australia, 2015.

Memoir (for children):
Yes, I Can! Abdi's Story, by Abdi Aden, self-
published, Australia, 2018.

A poem:

Home, by Warsan Shire, United Kingdom, 2011.

⁕ In writing: http://austinrefugees.org/home-a-refugee-poem/

⁕ Audio read by Warsan Shire: http://seekershub.org/blog/2015/09/home-warsan-shire/

TAKE ACTION

The orphanage 'Bright Dream' does not exist. However, many organisations around the world are doing amazing work to support human rights. You can find out more here:

⁕ http://www.roads-to-refuge.com.au

⁕ https://www.amnesty.org.uk/junior-urgent-action-network

⁕ http://www.unhcr.org/en-au/

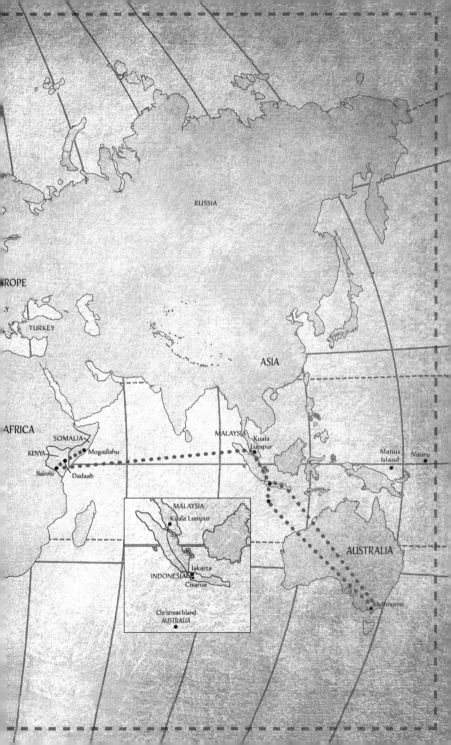

ACKNOWLEDGEMENTS

ABOVE ALL ELSE, I kiss the toes of the magnificent Hani Abdile: poet, survivor and superstar. I feel so lucky that our paths crossed. My world is richer from your laughter and stories, and you blew air into the lungs of this book. Thank you, thank you, thank you.

Deep respect to Abdi Aden: a kind and generous person with true integrity, who was a great sounding-board and advisor. Nadia Niaz also gave rich and thoughtful advice from a Muslim perspective.

So many people have trusted me with their stories – too many to name here, but especially detainees at the Pontville Immigration Detention Centre, and students in the Young Adult Migrant Education program at TAFE. I hope that you find all the freedom and happiness you deserve, and more.

I'm lucky to count among my friends a crack team of refugee advocates, including Clarissa Adriel, Janet Galbraith, Justine Davis, Mark Isaacs, Frederika Steen, Pamela Curr and Kirsty Madden, who have all inspired and advised me on this project and many others. Thank you, too, to all the tireless people around the world who work for organisations such as Amnesty and the UNHCR to bring about a better, more just world.

The birth scene was given the seal of midwife's approval by my wonderful friend Nina Cadman. Steve Mushin applied his neverending curiosity, enthusiasm and imaginative genius to this project – everyone needs at least one Steve in their life, and I'm very grateful I have mine.

Thank you to my editor, Elise Jones, who has showed superhuman levels of dedication in bringing the first two books of this series to print at the same time. You really have 'touched the sun'! Erica Wagner, my publisher at Allen & Unwin, has been wise and wonderful as always. I really struck gold with the whole team at Allen & Unwin – being published by you is an honour.

My beautiful family, you are the honey in my tea. Actually, you're also the tea, and the milk, and the cup itself. Pretty much everything. I love you.

ABOUT THE AUTHOR

EMILY CONOLAN IS a writer and teacher, who is also known for her humanitarian work. For her role in establishing a volunteer support network for asylum seekers in Tasmania, she has been awarded Tasmanian of the Year, Hobart Citizen of the Year, and the Tasmanian Human Rights Award. The stories of courage and resilience she has heard in the course of her work with refugees, combined with tales from her own family history, inspired her to write the Freedom Finders series.